Words Come Alive

OrangeBooks Publication

Website: www.orangebooks.in

First Edition 2025

ISBN: 978-93-6554-007-9

Price: Rs. 350.00

Printed in India

Words Come Alive

Mounting a Love Campaign

VEEKSHA VAGMITA

OrangeBooks Publication
www.orangebooks.in

This Novel is Dedicated to Love: Our Only Hope in a World Beset by Darkness

Contents

Chapter 1

She is the Boss

"This has to be done," Divya screamed on the phone. Divya was generally screaming on the phone. Those reluctantly working under her, always cowering before her, dutifully bootlicking her, preferred the word "holler". The word was favoured over every other synonym, and there was a fascinating story behind its meteoric rise to fame.

Here's how the story goes. It was just another crazy day two years ago. Divya had reprimanded an employee with such unsparing ferocity that the entire office received a jolt. Glances were exchanged rapidly and everyone's face looked like a question mark. The office echoed with the unspoken question: "What the hell just happened?" Well, it didn't take very long for the mystery to be revealed.

The door to Divya's cabin opened slowly. Basu—the target of the boss's renowned rage—stumbled out. There was nothing unusual in Divya having an outburst. She was like an explosive that could blow up anytime. Her employees had resigned themselves to daily insults since they couldn't afford to leave their job, or at least that is what they had come to believe. Among Divya's many unenviable talents was her complete mastery of mind games. She had disarmed her employees slowly and strategically till she had gained tight control over them. Now they all danced to her tune. They had forgotten that they had a right to politely differ if they were not on the same page as her. They wouldn't even mutter their objection to Divya's appalling sense of proportion, reflected in her penchant for making a tower out of a toyshop.

The employees had nearly, but not entirely, made peace with their customary ill-treatment. It was such a pity that their spirit of adaptation won them no praise from either their boss or anyone else. If anything, it gave rise to an existential crisis. Accepting arbitrary tyranny stripped their life of substance and meaning. Now they needed to find a way to *live with themselves*, believing they were *worth something*. Unless they held on to some sense of pride, how could they get on with their miserable life? To preserve their self-worth, they convinced themselves that they were just another set of employees overawed by a difficult boss. What was so disastrous about that? God knows how many employees in organisations all over the globe faced the same predicament! So, things were not so bad after all—a consolation that kept them from collapsing in a heap of self-loathing.

Divya had spun a fine web in which all her employees were hopelessly trapped. No one had dared to put in their papers even in such a preposterous situation. Even if a resignation was handed over, it would be enormously difficult to escape Divya's clutches. You could be released, of course. *But only if she willed it so.*

The employees in this office were little better than automatons. Or, perhaps, that is not entirely accurate. They were, in fact, worse off. Those machines had to simply follow instructions—nothing more, nothing less. But the employees were never given clear commands, creating a storm of confusion. The wildly varying instructions could put to shame the capricious weather and even Divya's ever-changing figure. The commands were changed, revised, reworked, and then changed again—all in the span of a single day. The tasks assigned to the employees were rather peculiar. They could be told to ascertain the exact number of mannequins that would attract the maximum customers to a shop selling apparel. Or, they could be ordered to find out the colour of the shirts that sold the most in spring. The goal was to find a sure-fire way to revive failing enterprises, but there was no method to this business.

For Divya, however, nothing could be amiss in the enterprise she had built with the sheer force of her will. She had named her business Spicy Solutions: "The place you visited not for airy-fairy notions but for perfect resolutions to your business conundrums."

****

The employees took great pains to ensure that no scraps from the juicy material in wide circulation trickled into their conversations with Divya. If she got a whiff of a dramatic scene being discussed with great relish behind her back, she would burst into flames. Any reminder of her daily theatrics gnawed at her Conscience, which was mighty scared of Guilt and ran helter-skelter to evade it. Once Guilt got so fed up with this dysfunctional Conscience that it screamed out: "Bastard, you are supposed to let me in if you have any intention of doing your bloody job, but it looks like you couldn't care less. All the Consciences part of your ilk make way for me even if I prick them a little. That's because inducing guilt for wrong deeds is their job description. You, on the other hand, spend all your energy trying to ward me off. You single-handedly exhaust me more than any other Conscience I have encountered so far. Nothing about you even remotely makes sense. First, your lethargy is of legendary proportions: Who runs away from a job that is the reason for their very existence? Second, you act in the strangest manner possible: every action of yours betrays your lunacy. Third, you've become compromised: this is not an uncommon occurrence but even here you're setting new records. What bothers me most are the signs that you're simply masquerading as a Conscience. If that's the case, you better run before it's too late."

Guilt couldn't be blamed for his frustration. Divya's Conscience had been twisted out of shape, warped beyond recognition, and made to forget his job description. No wonder, he behaved oddly and did nothing at all. Deep down, Divya knew the unvarnished truths about her beguilingly polished personality. But she never allowed them to rise to the surface lest Guilt came unbidden along with them. She had a simple coping mechanism: keep Guilt at bay and everything will go her way. As long as she could elude or, even better, vanquish Guilt, she could do anything she pleased. And she always did what she pleased. If she couldn't do it herself, she arm-twisted others to meet her outlandish demands. If anyone committed the grave offence of calling what was crazy "crazy", she would rip the moron to shreds. She would stab at his self-esteem till he believed himself to be the imbecile he was being made out to be. Divya would cure him of his rebelliousness with one merciless tirade. Once the task was done and over with, she nipped Guilt in the bud the way she would crush a cigarette butt with her stilettos.

She never thought about the tirades that kept her employees in a state of terror. Even their animated conversations had an undertone of fear. Divya's Memory never retained anything that would allow Guilt to creep in. Her Memory was adept at wiping out things she didn't wish to recall. Divya had a mantra that was simple, simpler than simple—oh, it was so wonderfully simple that it was simply absurd:

What was done was done. It was in the past. It was history. In fact, it never even happened.

So, if an employee made the fatal error of bringing up something that had been consigned to oblivion, he unknowingly gave Guilt a chance to raise its scary head. And Divya couldn't bear it when the tentacles of Guilt wrapped themselves around her. To set herself free, she hurled accusation after accusation at the employee till she was perfectly convinced of her pristine innocence and the devilry of the person before her. Guilt sank back into the murky depths of her being. The employee, though blameless like a newborn babe, was racked by guilt that was not his own.

The abject obedience of the employees did little to save them from Divya's fury. Not a day passed without someone accidently touching one of her million raw nerves. The fallout of such a blunder can be easily imagined.

****

Coming back to that dramatic day two years ago, poor Basu had become a punching bag for Divya. His deathly pale face and shaky legs gave his co-workers the distinct impression that he had just seen a ghost and was reeling from the shock. With practised stealth, they stole a glance at him every now and then. But no one dared to meet his gaze. When eyes meet, there is almost a chemical reaction. Sympathy, buried within, shoots up to the surface. And sympathy, however subtle, was heresy in this office. So, the employees tucked their emotions behind a mask of indifference—resisting the urge to get up from their seats and help the poor guy get to his desk. Performing even this simple task was a spectacular feat in an office so cold, it would leave you shivering in the peak of summer. If you were spotted displaying sympathy for the "scoundrel" Divya had gleefully cut down to size, you would be given an earful that would paralyse you for the rest of the day. Solidarity and sympathy had no place in this office. They had to be choked, buried, disguised, murdered—whatever it took to escape Divya's wrath, which was always a trigger away. And the triggers were so many that even God would've gone mad trying to keep count of them.

Basu's only fault was that he had gone up to Divya just when she needed a dustbin for her emotional debris. Every day, muck was flung in every direction and no one even whimpered in protest. Every day, one person had the misfortune of being in Divya's vicinity when she needed to unleash the beast in her. Basu bemoaned his bad luck.

****

The enigmatic enterprise conceived and controlled by Divya seemed like a domain that was specially designed for Fear. In other workplaces, Courtesy, Cooperation, Collaboration and all the bloody Cs were placed on a pedestal. But, in Spicy Solutions, Fear had the clout befitting a royal personage. Divya herself was fear incarnate. Curiosity snatched the reins from Fear whenever he was not looking. She would then direct the office conversations towards forbidden subjects. The employees often got caught discussing subjects supposed to be off-limits within the office premises. That's when Trouble landed. This was his moment. He gloried in his importance. Divya, too, would be in top form at a moment like this. There was nothing she enjoyed more than taking people to task. She would look at the guilt-ridden employees with part anger, part amusement. Her anger was palpable, but she didn't allow her body language to betray her amusement. That would dilute the seriousness of their transgression. Stony silence descended on the offenders like a blanket cutting off air supply. If that was not suffocating enough, Divya slipped a metaphorical noose onto their neck. She would tighten the noose with a deadly scowl that left them gasping for breath. This scowl was a precursor to the severe rebuke awaiting them in her cabin, famously called the torture chamber.

****

Basu staggered towards his desk with superhuman effort, looking around the room with pleading eyes. But his treacherous colleagues buried their heads in their files, making a show of being terribly busy. That performance had become second nature to them. Even if there was an earthquake, they would have remained glued to their seats with their unseeing eyes fixed on their files. The sight of them evoked the image of scared mice. If Divya saw them whiling away their time, they were done for. You could never predict when she would materialize and pin you to the wall with her razor-sharp eyes. The employees had a hazy notion of what they were doing, but they enacted their part well enough to get their salary. *So, why on earth would they interrupt their performance, the source of their livelihood, by helping Basu reach his desk? After all, how difficult was it to make your way to your bloody desk even if your legs were trembling? Okay, fine. Even if your* feeble *legs were trembling* uncontrollably. *How many times had they told Basu to go for a brisk walk every day? Neglecting his health had made Basu as flimsy as a leaf that could be swept away by even a gentle breeze. Was that their fault?* The employees felt mighty confident of the reasonableness of their decision to be unhelpful. And yet, their conscience was uneasy. So, they built the argument inside their heads even further. Not that they all thought alike. But there were common strands in their thought process since they could make only so many excuses to justify their obnoxious behaviour. They persisted in denying their guilt. *What was the worst that could happen, huh?* A predictable defence for all errors of omission. *He may have lost his balance … and perhaps dropped to the floor … maybe with a thud, maybe a violent thud … maybe more than once …* Now they were beginning to get overpowered by remorse. They gave Basu furtive glances and felt the difficulty of giving the matter a favourable spin—a spin that ensured the verdict of the universe was in their favour, even if their impractical conscience called them sinners. They were inwardly wrestling with their conscience. *At worst, he will twist an ankle or hurt a knee. That's not going to kill him, is it? No, he won't break his hipbone. No, he won't bang his head against anything if his legs give way. No, he won't have a concussion. No, he won't be wounded by this betrayal. Wait. Wait. This is not a* betrayal. *No, it is not. I told you it is not. Oh, just shut up and listen. He may suffer a minor injury—the keyword here is "minor"—and that would be unfortunate. But it's not like the world would come to an end! Stumbling, tottering, swaying, praying—he will eventually reach his desk, which is not in another continent. So, this rascal should not be playing on people's sympathies by looking so despondent. Does he not know our constraints? Was he born yesterday? He's not performing a herculean task, and he should stop making it look like one.*

Basu did manage to reach his desk but only after losing his balance and falling a few—to be precise, fifteen—times. It was obviously no cause for great alarm. People stumbled and fell all the time. But they picked themselves up without making a hullabaloo. So did Basu. He, however, got no credit for maintaining a dignified demeanour despite the embarrassing falls in full public view. His colleagues kept justifying their cruel passivity to their guilty conscience. *Far worse things have happened in the world! There has got to be some sense of proportion.* They desperately tried to fight off their mounting guilt, but to no avail.

Harassed by Guilt. Fettered by Fear. The employees were at the end of their tether.

****

Fear was a tyrant. He sealed your lips when you were dying to speak. But then there were other forces like Curiosity. Though Fear could easily overpower Curiosity when he was in his element, the latter had her sneaky ways of getting her job done. When Fear, too secure of his dominion, was not surveying his kingdom, Curiosity wormed her way into the minds of the employees, who had been enslaved by him. Once she got in, she slyly edged out Fear, who was always so busy flexing his muscles that he failed to notice Curiosity's slight nudges. If he managed to notice, Curiosity batted her eyelids at him like a coquette, distracting him long enough to expel him from his own territory. When Fear returned to his senses, he looked around and thundered: "What the hell just happened?" Curiosity, hidden from view, watched him with gloating satisfaction. But she wasted no time in getting to work. She knew Fear would snatch back his kingdom soon enough.

****

Fear may have been a force to be reckoned with, but Curiosity was no pushover. Before Fear could re-establish his rule, Curiosity gripped everyone in the office. She goaded them to draw out the details about Basu's nightmarish experience inside the torture chamber. As Curiosity rose to a crescendo, Fear dwindled into a pale shadow. He helplessly watched the employees dancing to Curiosity's tune.

Feeling bold, everyone shook off Fear the Tyrant and gathered around the black-sheep celebrity of the day. Basu found himself fenced in from all sides, which seemed rather menacing. But he didn't panic. For two reasons. First, he couldn't possibly be more frightened than he already was. Second, he knew from experience the irrepressible need for entertainment in a workplace resembling a prison: the only exception was that the inmates had lodged themselves in it of their own "free will", little knowing, or knowing all too well, though they would die before they admitted it, that they were no better than captives, however much they flaunted their designation. Their survival depended on how cleverly they deceived themselves, investing their wispy identities with immense significance. Who could blame them for this psychological trickery? If they were courageous, no, crazy enough to embrace their real identities, they would've felt like jumping out of their own skin. They had to believe they were something, someone, anyone—but not *captives, certainly not captives,* even if they were *exactly that.* They needed the illusion of having some agency. This make-believe may seem silly but, in a way, it was necessary for those imprisoned souls being bulldozed, day in and day out. Without this fiction, things would have fallen apart. The centre could hold because the illusion was as solid as a rock. And that wasn't so bad after all.

For human beings, the loss of freedom is probably their worst nightmare. But when the *unthinkable* happens, and it happens rather often, though in varying degrees, they reframe the situation with astonishing speed. Reality is stopped in its tracks before it can come close enough to sink in. Oh, how good we are at dodging Reality! It's one of those things we do with such incredible ease. So, we need not wonder at modern-day slaves thinking highly of themselves. No one is willing to accept slavery, and yet there are slaves aplenty. They just don't look the part. Slavery has assumed a different guise in today's world. Modern-day slaves, dressed smartly, smiling wanly, slogging cheerlessly, have nothing to lose but a façade of respectability and an appearance of competence. Or let's say it straight: They've nothing to lose but the illusion that they are not in chains. They talk about their "servitude" every now and then, but it is always in a jocular manner. They might be spared the indignities of slavery in its ancient sense, but they are oppressed all the same. More often than not, employers treat them as a dumping ground for work that keeps piling on. If they burn out and fail to perform—it's a miracle if they don't! —they are viewed as a spent force and nudged towards the door.

Basu wore the look of a slave longing to throw off his shackles and run away. He was, however, held back by something he could feel but not define. Was it a masochistic attachment to his own bondage? Or, an acquired sense of powerlessness that made this traumatic job seem as inescapable as fate?

The captives in this office hid behind a cloak of respectability contrived by a performance that made them look important, even if no one was looking. The employees would put on their professional mask and go through the contents of their files with a look of deep concentration. They reread sentences with a furrowed brow, chasing their meaning like a mirage. Exhausted, they checked random trivia with blithe indifference; it was the concentrated essence of pure nonsense. Whenever they examined the files, their mind felt like a sieve incapable of holding on to any information. Everything fell through the cracks: some of it was lost instantly, while the rest emptied out gradually. Not that it made any difference. The content was like loose sand. Even if you grabbed a fistful, it would slip away like a thief afraid of being found out. They would sign the files with a flourish: the only enjoyable part of the dreary performance. Deep down, they felt disgusted with this daily farce. They were learning nothing new and forgetting all they did know. They were murdering time and insulting their intelligence by peering at bogus files. Their repository of knowledge had been lying on the shelf ever since they joined this office. If things went on like this, a time would come when Divya could legitimately call them fools. But, how would they level up if they couldn't escape Divya's constant scrutiny?

Divya could detect the artifice in their style of working, but she cared only about the output. Or rather, she hardly cared about the output. Still, she would throw a fit if she didn't get exactly what she wanted. And that happened all the time since what she wanted was never clearly defined. The employees spent most of their time shooting the breeze. If a "serious" task was assigned to them, they switched to shooting darts in the dark. On a lucky day, they would hit the mark. But those occasions were few and far between. Most of the time, they were berated for their incompetence. They had to perform the same task umpteen times before they got Divya's reluctant nod of approval.

****

Let's return to the drama of *that* day two years ago. Basu's colleagues were itching to know what had transpired in Divya's room. They might never get a complete picture of the work they did, but they could at least amuse themselves with a vivid picture of the sideshows at their workplace. As a matter of fact, the sideshows often took centre stage, making the real work look like an afterthought or a digression. The employees were egging Basu on with their eyes but were afraid to spell out the burning question. Vinay, an overzealous soul, took the plunge. He released the caged words into the air in a voice intended to be a whisper, just loud enough for the huddled employees to hear. But his vocal cords had a will of their own. The hall resounded with the words: "What the hell just happened?" Everyone froze with fright. Mixed with the fright was muted anger. Why couldn't Vinay ever hold his slippery tongue or lower his volume when he was blurting something out! For five minutes, no one spoke, stirred, or even breathed loudly. When nothing happened, they knew they were safe. Divya had gone for a cup of tea and wouldn't be back before an hour. They were free birds, at least for now. So, they resumed their conversation. Vinay had given voice to the question bouncing on the tip of everyone's tongue. What the hell had happened that made Basu almost seem like an apparition? The employees were wonderstruck. Divya had surpassed herself. Even tyranny had degrees, and Divya always aimed high. So, she kept raising the bar for tyrannical behaviour. Since terrorising people was her forte, she had to scale ever greater heights of tyranny to show her unstoppable progress to her own self. Today, the bar had touched the sky, as evidenced by Basu's pitiable state. His colleagues were dying to know every single detail of the goings-on in the torture chamber, caring little about the consequences of extracting information that was supposed to be forbidden. In their mind's eye, they could see the barbs Divya would have directed at Basu with oozing contempt, the jibes she must have flung at him like a resounding slap, the expletives that would have punctuated her tirade, the slips she must have rubbed in his face with sadistic satisfaction, the killer expression she would have maintained all through the performance, the pleasure she must have derived from every blow that landed in the right place, and finally, the "mission accomplished" look that would have declared the end of the torment. These mental images whetted their appetite for the real story. They were hungry for the cornucopia of revelations they could feast on for a long time to come.

Basu didn't want to rob his drooling colleagues of this rare treat. He clumsily mouthed the word "horror". His lips were stiff and his throat was parched. Though he willed his vocal cords to obey, no sound issued from his lips. Another colleague, emboldened by Curiosity's growing power, joined in. Dispensing with the obligatory question "Are you okay?", he came directly to the point: "What the hell just happened?" As if on cue, everyone, flinging away the last remnants of Fear, said in a jarring chorus: "*Arre bhai*, what the hell just happened?". Though the jittery Basu quietly revelled in all the attention he had attracted, he was uncomfortable with being the cynosure of all stares. Eyes bore into him, seeking to ferret out as many delicious details as possible. Well, Basu didn't wish to disappoint them despite the knot of worry forming inside him. He could court trouble by letting out information he was supposed to keep entirely to himself. It was an unwritten rule that whatever happened inside the torture chamber *stayed* inside the torture chamber. But that was too much to expect from employees in dire need of comic relief. Well, they got plenty of it. It took some time for Basu's voice to make a comeback but it returned with a bang. His theatrical account of his tribulations in the torture chamber was nothing less than a showstopper. Basu narrated his traumatic experience with unusual flair and breathtaking candour. Enraged by all the humiliation, he roared like a wounded tiger: "I have *self-respect. Everyone has self-respect.* That's not going to change even if it is something Divya conveniently forgets." There was a pause before he resumed with renewed fervour, "I have *feelings. Everyone has feelings.* But that lady cares for nobody's feelings except her own. Is she a human shark posing as one of us?" That was intense. And highly entertaining. Basu's account of Divya's record-breaking theatrics had been so hilarious that his colleagues laughed till their sides ached. It was a devilishly funny story that the employees never grew tired of discussing. Although they knew it all by heart, the story always produced much mirth. When laughter erupted anywhere in the office, it was obvious what was being recounted.

Even on a bleak day, everyone beamed at the mention of that darkly comic episode and its rib-tickling horror. What's even more remarkable is that Divya, with all her sharpness, never detected the story that was the staple of office gossip. Not a day passed when it wasn't discussed more than once. But it fell below her radar and was never within her hearing. That was quite a feat.

It looked like the employees were determined to not let Divya ruin this source of endless delight. And they succeeded in keeping their favourite funny story under wraps. Divya never got a whiff of it. Who would've thought that this frightened bunch would be smart enough to escape Divya's relentless scrutiny!

Well, people have their ways of surviving tyranny.

****

So much happened on that legendary day two years ago that it cannot be cramped into the canvas of a single chapter. For now, it is enough to know that this was one hell of a day. Holler became a code among the employees, edging out Scream, Yell, Shout and others of his ilk. It was also the day when Holler and Horror turned into sworn enemies. Fear, Horror's greatest ally, never missed an opportunity to take a dig at Holler for behaving like a self-important buffoon. That day was etched in Curiosity's memory. Overflowing with pride, she had pronounced it as the day of victory. That day, she had *completely taken over* the employees, leaving *no space at all* for Fear in their minds. It was the day she had broken all her records. Little did she know the rapid descent that would follow this towering accomplishment.

From that day on, Holler conveyed a world of meaning, though it was not yet reflected by the dictionary. "But then, who cares about dictionaries?" Holler would say rhetorically. *Words are not in the dictionary; words are in the mind*—he would borrow from Virginia Woolf to hit back at Fear when he tried to show him his place. "Only the damned elite use the word Holler, but Fear is an integral part of every person's dictionary. You are the word of choice for a chosen few, but I'm in wide circulation in every community all the year round. So, don't put on airs because you're bandied about by a bunch of losers," roared Fear when he saw the smug look on Holler's face. Holler had his reasons to feel important. Every time he was uttered by someone, it elicited chuckles and knowing looks. He seemed to have finally arrived. The world outside may be indifferent to his accomplishment. So what? He was prized in his own domain, and no one could dispute that claim.

Chapter 2

Horror and Holler: An Epic Rivalry

That eventful day two years ago had set the stage for the rivalry between Horror and Holler. In fact, it had led to the formation of rival camps. Fear sided with Horror, while Curiosity joined the opposite camp even though she had no soft spot for Holler. The reason for that was simple. She would *never* be on the same side as Fear because he seemed to have made it his business to subdue Curiosity in the minds of the employees. Killing Curiosity was not Fear's mandate by any stretch of the imagination. He was just supposed to leave a chilling effect that would rob people of their peace, appetite, sleep, and preferably, their power to think. But Fear focused all his energies on crushing Curiosity even before it was fully awakened in the minds of the employees. Whenever Curiosity tried to slip into Fear's terrain, she had to beat a humiliating retreat. He would sense Curiosity's nearness and motives with an unerring instinct. Determined to thwart her efforts, he would go into overdrive. "Danger! Danger! Danger!" would start buzzing inside the heads of the employees, making them frightened of their own inquisitiveness. This dealt a deadly blow to Curiosity, who was fast fading into irrelevance. But Curiosity was not going to take this lying down. She could be a bitch when rubbed the wrong way. It won't be long before Fear found that out. She would make him repent his wicked deeds. She would wipe that triumphant grin off his face. Just wait and see.

She aligned herself with Holler as if that was the most natural thing to do. Since Holler was not blessed with self-awareness, he was perfectly convinced that it was his charm that drew Curiosity to him. This was a boost to his vanity. Curiosity guessed the silly idea entertained by Holler when he welcomed her with a flirtatious wink. His flamboyance almost made her wince, but she kept her face impassive lest she bruised his ego and made another enemy. She let him hold on to his illusions. Even if she had tried to enlighten him, he wouldn't have listened. Illusions had the power to keep you going. They made you feel special even if you were strikingly ordinary. They made you feel worthy even if you had done nothing to prove your value. They made you feel distinct even if no one ever looked at you twice. In short, they kept you going. Curiosity was too driven to need illusions for motivation. But Holler would have come undone if his illusions were snatched from him. So, she let him make a song and dance about attracting her. No one paid much attention to him, so he could spout whatever nonsense he wanted. She was determined to not get provoked by his buffoonery. After all, who knew what lay ahead? Even a daft fellow like Holler could be of help in getting even with Fear, who was acting way too smart for his own good.

With time, more words joined one or the other camp. This development coincided with an upheaval within the larger word-community, which was once bound together within the confines of a dictionary. Now this community was a fragmented bunch: many words fumed inside traps laid by stiff definitions. They burned with envy when their peers were invested with new and modern meanings. This gave those words a fresh lease of life and a dynamic personality. Well, they were damn lucky. Their good fortune infuriated the words who had been shoehorned into a rigid mould by definitions that allowed no room for play. They hated the bastards who had gained prominence they did nothing to earn but missed no opportunity to flaunt. These rascals boasted that their continuing relevance was a result of their malleability and inherent vastness. Their meaning could be easily remoulded or expanded to keep up with the changing times. For these words, bloated with self-importance, it all boiled down to a few indisputable facts, even if they were highly disputable—they were special; they were superior; they possessed in abundance what was conspicuously missing in their trapped peers. It seemed to them that their unfortunate peers were entirely to blame for their predicament. "Come on, let's face it. This is their own doing, and we don't need to be sympathetic to their follies," said one of the fortunate rascals. "What is their own doing?" asked one of the listeners, who was kindly disposed to his caged peers. Unable to come up with anything resembling an answer, the lucky bastard hastily concluded that the stagnation of other words had something to do with their very essence. He didn't care to elaborate further because he had nothing meaningful to say. The words incensed by his baseless comment looked around, ready to punch the daylights out of him. But he was nowhere to be found. Was he an apparition they had dreamed up together? He couldn't have vanished so fast unless he had literally melted into the air, which was simmering like a volcano. The words looked at each other in amazement.

There was a time when all the words were one big family. No one was big or small, ordinary or special, superior or inferior. That was when the word-community was a unified entity with a collective sense of belonging. But as the rest of the world got polarised, divided and fragmented, so did the word-community. The bulky dictionaries, once revered like a holy book, had become relics of the past. Their contents, once neatly packed into a tangible tome, had lost their materiality and were fast losing their sanctity. Now Google was the Bible, the dictionary and the force that kept the world turning. If you cared to look it up, the myriad meanings of a word would be splashed across your screen for a super-quick reference. Well, even that was inconvenient for the new generation. Given a choice, they would invent a language of their own: mutating idioms, murdering spellings, inventing new meanings, trifling with punctuation, and breaking all grammatical rules that restricted their freedom of expression. But even in the merry madness of the digital sphere, there were only so many liberties you could take with language, thanks to the purists, pedants, sticklers, editors, and language lovers attacked for living in the Middle Ages!

The words facing stagnation were mature enough not to wallow in misery. Adversity had had a salutary effect on them. They chose to count their blessings. At least they were in circulation, they mused soberly. No doubt, they had become stale—they themselves had to close their nose every now and then to escape their own stench. But then what was to be expected? Their meaning had remained the same and would probably never change. Funnily enough,

Same, Meaning and Change were among these stinky words. Still, they were lucky enough to have escaped the fate of their peers who had been stripped of all their self-esteem by being labelled "old-fashioned", "dated", "archaic", and the like. Though dictionaries themselves had been reduced to content floating around in cyberspace, diminishing their former stature and glory, they latched on to their residual authority by declaring words like Afeared and Hark out of use. Many words were either languishing on the margins or rotting in oblivion. The online dictionaries pronounced them outdated with cruel clarity. And then they were words like Impecunious, Imperturbable and Importune that were on nobody's lips. To be fair, they did find mention in some conversations once in a blue moon. The words had been granted the dubious honour of being "formal". Such formal words were no longer favoured by modern speakers, who liked conversations to be smooth and crisp. Big words often spoiled the flow of a dialogue. They were uncommon and lost on ordinary people. However, many erudite people had a secret liking for such words. But unless they were surrounded by people of their own kind, they swallowed these words before they escaped their lips lest they invited the charge of being "pompous" or, even worse, "uncool". They didn't really care if they were criticised for their pomposity. But to be called "uncool"! No, that couldn't be borne. That would be too much. Was there anything worse than being described as "uncool"? They could take it if they were called a "criminal". It would bother them, no doubt, but they would get over it after a nap or a drink or two. But the label of "uncool" would tear them apart.

Impish couldn't hide his amusement when the trio of Impecunious, Imperturbable and Importune would pass him by. Their drooping shoulders, eyes devoid of shine, sallow cheeks, slow strides, and a demeanour conveying a resigned acceptance of life—all of it made Impish newly aware of his "great luck", a term he always clarified with a mental footnote. Luck was not some random act of divine indulgence; it was a gift from the heavens to the ones found worthy of the good things in life. His great luck was proof that his worth had been certified by divine forces. He was perfectly justified in mocking his peers when the powers ruling the universe had themselves chosen to withhold luck from them. Even if that were not the case, he had no hesitation whatsoever in ridiculing his own peers because he, Impish, knew in his bones that he would *never* be in their position. That would never be *his* fate. He was in wide circulation among the educated members of society. There was *something* in him—he just couldn't pinpoint it—that would sustain his charm forever. He had the right to laugh at the losers who did nothing but mope around with a long face. Oh God, they were so pathetic!

Little did he know that he himself had become the laughingstock among many groups of the word-community. His habit of walking with his head held ridiculously high, almost as if he was reading an augury hidden in the sky, exposed him to much ridicule. "He thinks he's a seer," exclaimed Pretty. "That's exactly what he is: a *seer.* His gifts are limited to just seeing things, although he clearly fancies himself to be a soothsayer. His alleged clairvoyance has never alerted us to an approaching storm or assured us of good times to come. I always knew he was frivolous, flippant, fatuous—just a few of his follies—but now I feel that his greatest fault is his fakeness." Such a fine critique by the revered Knowledge was followed by respectful silence, giving everyone time to hold the thought. After a suitable pause, Ditty added a note of levity to the conversation by reciting a poem:

Gazing pointlessly at a perfectly clear sky

The pretentious Impish passed us by

Maybe he was searching for the divine eye

Or just hoping to find some apple pie

He found neither but bumped into Trouble

And received the lesson of his life

Impish became peevish

But that came as no surprise

He got what he richly deserved

Everyone agreed it served him right.

The poem lightened the mood and received lavish praise. Ditty's face glowed as she accepted the compliments graciously.

But Impish lived in his own world. He was willing to bear the daily neck aches brought on by tilting his head upwards if it dissociated him from the miserable trio with whom he shared the first three letters. He wanted to advertise his importance to preclude the possibility of appearing in the same sentence as his pitiable peers. And holding his head too high was his peculiar way of announcing his higher stature. He had a mortal terror of being grouped with his unlucky peers and, like them, turning into an object of pity. Well, he didn't turn into an object of pity but became a butt of jokes.

There was another reason he needed to hold his *too* high *all the time*. He harboured a secret desire to gain entry to the exclusive club of the elite among the word-community. The most prominent among them were Dignity, Fraternity, Humanity, Sustainability, Beauty and Sovereignty. These words had the stature of dignitaries and the reputation for being quintessential snobs. They soared above the hoi polloi in the word-community and didn't even deign to glance at anyone below their rank. He felt slighted by their utter obliviousness to his existence. Reality, the ultimate killjoy, reminded him of his middling stature. But that did little to dent his exaggerated self-worth, which was probably not such a bad thing. A serious reality check might have been the death of him. He needed his illusion of superiority: it was the one thing that could save him if the world came crashing down. And soon enough, it would. But it was unclear if the illusion would come to his rescue.

****

Though the regal attitude of the bigwigs enraged Impish, he wished to insinuate himself into their league by looking the part so well that he would be accepted as one of them. It was a remote possibility but what was the harm in dreaming? Impish was acutely aware of the impossibility of a generous welcome. Unless you matched up to their status, you stood no chance of gaining entry into their closely guarded league. Still, Impish coveted a membership to this club and would have grovelled before the VIPs to be allowed a place in it. It was his pride that saved him from sacrificing his dignity by such self-abasement. A part of him derided them all as elitist jerks, but the desire to belong where he *did not* belong was too strong to keep him from committing some folly.

He began preparing for the subterfuge in earnest. Though the undertaking was doomed to failure—he would be caught in no time—there was no stopping this train-wreck adventure. Though anyone could see he was a pathetic wannabe, he had a dim notion, or rather an illusion, that he was good enough to fit into this league. He didn't have that kind of status but he had *himself*. He was *Impish*. What greater qualification was needed? High on vanity, which he kept fuelling by self-praise, he had begun to entertain the idea that felt his very being was proof of his status. In the grip of his delusion, he mimicked the demeanour of an emperor and thundered at an imaginary audience, "Those condescending fools fail to see that I'm *not* their equal; I am *far superior*. They will never come up to my level. I'm the *greatest of all*. I am *God's chosen word*. I am *Impish*. For heaven's sake, I am *Impish*. Don't they know who I am?" His sense of superiority had assumed comic proportions. Not surprisingly, his plan of action reflected that grandiosity:

When he got there, he would pretend to be more at ease than those who actually belonged. Confidence would ooze from every pore of his being; a smile would flicker over his lips if he received a nod from a passerby; he would take in the minutiae of the place with a gaze trained to convey deep familiarity; he would shake hands with everyone like it was a daily ritual he knew how to perform better than them. More than anything, he would look everyone in the eye with a jovial expression, as befitted an enduring camaraderie. He would draw the VIPs into a conversation of his liking and shut down any interruptions while he was talking. He would command their full attention, elicit their admiration even if it required intimidation, and call out anyone who didn't respect the decorum expected when a king was speaking to his subjects.

Well, things could go in only two directions. Despite his glaring lack of self-awareness, he was good at predicting the outcome of events. He could visualise with a fair degree of accuracy the way things would unfold, foreseeing the actions and reactions of those involved, including himself. It's a mystery how his messed-up mind could keep its grip on reality.

The worst-case scenario had a greater probability—the very thought sent shudders down Impish's spine. The real members would sniff him out (Lord have mercy!), grab him by the scruff of the neck (No! No! No!), sternly pronounce him an interloper (Oh, what a shame!), and unceremoniously dump him at the nearest vacant spot (What a bloody mess!). The second possibility was little better than wishful thinking, but Impish wasn't going to give up without trying. In this case, the snobs would get sucked into a bog of confusion by his unsettling composure, call into question their knowledge of who were their own peers, wonder if he was bluffing or if *they* were guilty of trespassing, clutch their heads in bewilderment, so convincing would be Impish's performance. This would clear the pathway for Impish to install himself in the world of the elite, turning into reality his wildest dreams. He was absolutely certain that he would, in no time, pick up all the mannerisms of the VIPs. But then, anything is possible in your wildest dreams.

****

Below the bigwigs was the class that had escaped mediocrity but fallen a little short of earning the distinction of being VIPs. Scintillating, bewitching, serendipity and magnificence were some of the words that had almost touched the zenith of popularity while remaining distinct from their run-of-the-mill peers. They were high-flying words who acted like they had arrived but secretly aspired to reach the top of the social ladder. They were almost there. But "almost" wasn't enough. In fact, it was even embarrassing to have risen so high and yet failed to touch the pinnacle of the social pyramid. To hide that subtle sense of inferiority, they made it a point to pat each other on the back with excessive zeal if there happened to be any kind of audience to watch their clumsy performance. Even after gaining a degree of social prominence that many words desperately wished to attain, they were plagued by insecurity. Having reached so close to the top and far above from the grassroots, they were terrified of losing their halo, especially when the words lower in rank eyed them with intense envy. They congratulated each other all too often, pitying their peers to show themselves luckier by comparison. This vanity show impressed no one and occasionally elicited derisive laughter. Language was becoming a maddeningly chaotic and fiercely competitive arena.

****

The words at Spicy Solutions reflected the divisiveness within their larger eco-system. Members of both the camps were always at loggerheads, if only for the heck of it. Each camp seemed to be a picture of unity, but then appearances are only appearances. Though the words waxed lyrical about the "strength in numbers" and the "power of oneness", their loyalty was actually sustained by a secret desire to serve their own interests while working for their camp. To avoid suspicion, they made an ostentatious display of every little thing they did for their team, even if it wasn't worthy of notice.

****

Holler had gained the kind of prominence he hardly deserved. Whereas Fear and Horror had been working hard to scare people for centuries,

Holler was missing from most people's vocabularies. So, people screamed and yelled, but very few were said to have hollered. While Holler sat idly on people's tongues, willing them to let him out for a change, Fear and Horror were running around with not a moment to spare. Their schedule might have been hectic, but the efforts they made were amply compensated by the endless merriment they afforded. It was so damn easy to scare people. No one knew better than Fear and Horror the profusion of wimps, often masquerading as macho men, in the world. Nor was there any dearth of comical situations that led to shrieking, howling, collapsing, hiding, running, and all manner of ridiculous responses. The creaking of a window would make people jump out of bed and scream at the top of their lungs as if a ghost had appeared before them. The entire neighbourhood was jolted out of slumber just like that. And it didn't even stop there. The matter was discussed for days on end. Every detail was dissected with utmost seriousness, which masked the pleasure derived from such a whole-hearted indulgence in gossip. The apparition that never appeared would spawn many stories and, at times, even become a legend. Despite such extreme fascination, this staple of daily conversations would fall out of favour the moment another unusual occurrence hogged the limelight.

Aware of the well-concealed cowardice of muscle-flexing men, Fear would sneak into their brains and set off alarm bells loud enough to freeze them with fright or send them running out of the house in the middle of the night. Sometimes they would come out on the streets stark naked, raving like madmen about some paranormal nonsense. Fear would relate these incidents to Horror, Fright and Shock—friends who were thick as thieves—with much relish, eliciting peals of laughter.

No one could deny Horror's prevalence, and by extension, significance, in a world where danger lurked in every corner, pandemonium reigned supreme, closely guarded secrets found a way to reveal themselves, haunted houses lived up to their name, skeletons in some cupboard tumbled out every other day, among many other occasions where Horror held sway.

Not every word managed to perch comfortably on people's tongues. Many words faced the accusation of being outworn and outdated—an accusation they flung back on to the humans who overused them to the point of obsolescence. Their protests fell on deaf ears as they were heartlessly dumped into the graveyard of language by editors known to be fastidious (the word community called them "fascists"). Words like "mollycoddle" and "gallivant" had once made their presence felt. They were now disparaged by the custodians of language as being rather old-fashioned. "But who made them the custodians of language?" asked the wounded words. They could be credited with having made their way into the vocabularies of speakers too many to be counted. Even if they had gone out of favour now, thanks to the famously moody and cranky human race, the words had once enjoyed *justified* popularity. But what on earth had Holler done to walk with a swagger befitting a king? He had neither gained much prominence after floating around pointlessly nor landed in the dustbin having achieved his share of glory. He was the epitome of mediocrity. Both Horror and Fear rolled their eyes whenever Holler passed them by. He didn't so much as glance in their direction, let alone give them a perfunctory nod of recognition. What made him think he had the right to be so conceited? He had simply become popular in an office that was conspicuously small and laughably quirky. And he had done nothing to earn even that useless distinction. It had happened purely by chance. But that didn't stop Holler from putting on airs. His importance in this office gave a real boost to his self-esteem. It made him feel like a word of immense significance. Not a day passed without someone mouthing or whispering things like "She's hollering again", "She's a holler queen", "When will she stop hollering at that poor chap?", "Even white noise can't drown out all this hollering", "I hope she doesn't holler at me" and other versions of statements emphasising the never-ending hollering that kept them strapped to their seats with an ear always cocked to catch faintest sound emerging from Divya's room. They had learned to identify the lull before the storm, the rumble before the bombardment, and the compliment before the well-rehearsed reprimand. They had turned dreadfully wary of her sugary smile declaring her intent to take the sting off her words, though, in reality, it amplified their effect by catching the listener off guard. And this was done by design. Always.

After that memorable day two years ago, "holler" conveyed everything that the employees wanted to say. It had actually become interchangeable with horror, with the employees muttering, "What a holler!", "She's a holler", "We're in a holler house!". Since it had become a code for the employees, everyone would suppress their chuckles whenever they heard the word "holler". Holler had happily broken free of the confines of his dictionary definition and turned into a word whose vibrancy kept growing with time.

Fear and Horror scoffed at him for luxuriating in fame that was bound to be short-lived and unlikely to extend beyond the confines of a cramped office with twenty employees. At times, they pitied him for his profound complacency and narrow horizons. Holler was not meant for great things. His glaring mediocrity would never lift him above all things ordinary. But Holler didn't seem to care, although he could dimly perceive what his rivals thought of him. He knew very well that he had no such thing as status in the word-community at large, but he refused to let it dampen his spirits. For him this office was the entire world. Dwelling and thriving in this office was what his existence had come to mean. He had made this place his permanent dwelling. He was too short-sighted to look beyond the present moment. In a way, that was a blessing. It freed him from nagging concerns about the future. That made it possible for him to soak in whatever was unfolding before his eyes. His mind was never clouded by worries. Oh, what a blessing it was to have a mind like a brilliantly clear sky! A mind so bereft of activity that it bore witness to its own stupidity!

Though his puny brain saved him the hassles of thinking about the future, it also failed to detect the signs of what lay ahead. So, he could never guess how the stories around him would unfold. It was beyond his power to anticipate the climax of a drama or the aftermath of a crisis. If he had had the slightest inkling of the colossal mess looming on the horizon, threatening to turn this pathetic workplace into a perfect madhouse, he would have bolted that very instant from the only place that ever gave him any importance. What's more, he would have been jauntily whistling a tune and coolly surveying the world outside just moments after he had exited the office premises. Just like he couldn't plan or foresee things, he had very little capacity to remember past events, even if it was something that happened a moment ago. To be realistic, his memory was not *that* faulty. He would often choose to dispel the fragments he recollected because it taxed his brain. And he didn't like to tax his brain. Well, that was Holler. He lived in the moment, swam with the current, pranced around when things went in his favour, vanished from view if reality seemed bitter—he was a silly creature.

****

"How did that happen?" asked Fear, who had earned the reputation for being forgetful. Not that he could help it. He was the embodiment of a feeling known for leaving people so muddled, frantic and confused that things would rapidly slip through even the tiniest cracks of their memory and their brain would be invaded by a mist that would obscure everything they could once recall in a heartbeat. Horror, who must have related the story a million times, gave a sigh. Although Horror, being a degree stronger than Fear, should've had no memory at all, he had devised a method to keep a record of things by writing them down in his diary. So, he once again turned to the page where he had jotted down the strange turn of events that had bestowed on Holler the Loser the accidental renown that he couldn't possibly take credit for. Holler, however, missed no opportunity to lay claim to his fortuitous fame. "Attention-hungry rascal!" hissed Horror. What had happened had happened. If he had made peace with what couldn't be undone, he wouldn't have grown so bitter. But he welcomed resentment and held it close to his heart. Soon enough, he had been consumed by malice. But then, Horror was all for being malicious. Peace and her ilk were far removed from the realm of his definition.

"Okay, I'll go over the events again. Listen carefully and try to hold on to at least something you hear. Start to memorise stuff if you have the propensity to forget things faster than one can say 'Yo'. So here we go. Again. Uff.

"On a cursed day two years ago, there was a tectonic shift in this workplace. Fortunes changed, rivalries emerged, an office legend took birth, our peers here got divided into camps, and Divya's Scream was no longer just a Scream. From that day on, she only hollered. Yell, Scream, Shout and Shriek soon left the building. They resurface every now and then, but seeing Holler's absolute reign, they turn back and go on a search for greener pastures. Holler, who used to sit idly in a corner most of the time, suddenly became a word that tickled everyone's imagination and brought an impish smile to their forlorn faces. The employees would titter and tattle the moment Divya blew her lid off. Everything she did was summed up in one word: Holler. Now the word signifies so many things that it's enough to just whisper it into someone's ear, and they will build an entire story from it. You know how shallow Holler is. All this has gone into his head, and he considers himself our equal. In his head, he probably thinks he's reached the pinnacle of popularity in the word-community. Who will tell him that his elevated status in this office has not made any difference to the guardians of language! No dictionary has even considered expanding or modifying his definition. When he had first set foot in this office, the words that had already made this place their home gave him such dirty looks, telling him with their eyes, frowns, hisses, sighs, and even the clatter of cups and plates to pick up his stuff and find another refuge. No one wanted him. No one. Still, the stubborn rascal settled in, although he did us the mercy of staying put in a spot that was thankfully hidden from view. I have heard that English-language speakers would have to use him, much against their will, when he sauntered into their heads uninvited. He literally danced inside their brains, compelling them to insert him into their sentences, even if it seemed terribly forced. The poor chaps would start getting dizzy and frantically compose a sentence that included Holler the Intruder, hoping to get rid of him by doing his bidding. But Holler would make things harder for the poor fellows. The rascal has perfected the art of getting on people's nerves or, in this case, their tongues. Just for some mean-spirited fun, he would sit on the tip of their tongue. This made it difficult for other words to get past him and be out into the open so that people could hear them being spoken. Word after word would push, kick, shove, and even punch Holler to create space, so that they could perform their job of enabling communication. That was supposed to be their job description, which this dumbass had merrily forgotten. Now this joker struts around like God's gift to language. Even the Hollers in other places have come specially to drill some sense into this idiot's head. Stories of his vainglory are spreading like wildfire in the word-community, making all the other Hollers, who are a picture of humility, the butt of jokes. As "our" Holler's insolence grows and grows, the jokes rapidly increase in number and become meaner than before. It's not just fellow Hollers who are exasperated with him; he has been getting on our nerves too. Isn't he, Fear? Isn't he? Jog your brains. How can you not remember … but let it be. You'll remember everything the moment you spot him walking on imaginary air. The very sight of him will give your brain the jolt it needs. It will all come back. I promise. So, can we leave the story here and trust that your brain will fill in the rest when Holler brings it back into action?" said Horror, knowing perfectly well that Fear couldn't bear a story to be abandoned midway. Fear won't let him breathe till he had narrated the full story in excruciating detail.

So, Horror resumed the narrative with a reluctance he didn't even try to conceal. His body language and lack of animation made his unwillingness to continue more than obvious. Fear was well-acquainted with Horror's ways of wriggling out of the task of storytelling. If Horror was smart, he was even smarter. He pretended not to notice anything, even though he took in every tiny detail of what transpired. He may have had an abysmal, almost dysfunctional, memory but that was amply compensated by his deft handling of whatever happened in the present. So, he listened coolly to Horror's lacklustre description of what happened *that day* two years ago. He prodded Horror with his eyes to throw some life into the story, but Horror was determined not to waste his energy on relating something that he would probably have to recount a thousand times more. He knew Fear would never work on his memory as long as he was spoon-fed stories. So, he inwardly resolved to make the story as dull as possible to discourage Fear from repeatedly asking him to recapitulate the same old story. But stories have a life of their own. And this story would always come alive even if you tried to murder it with a deadpan voice and colourless description. Even Horror was flummoxed when all of a sudden, the story began to tell itself. It flowed out of him of its volition.

… *Basu suddenly felt an urge to spit out everything he had been assaulted with. Divya's barbs, insults, mockery, you name it, came thick and fast and furious. They spun inside his head like a dervish. He felt too dizzy and dazed to string words together and form proper sentences. That was beyond him. He would need two days to relearn the art of making sentences. He could, however, communicate through fragments or just words. It turned out that he could do no better than mouth a single word, which was famously mistaken for a similar-sounding word. I was the word he was trying to let out but no sound came out. Sorry for killing the suspense but I must reveal beforehand that Holler was that similar-sounding son of a bitch. He hogged the limelight, just like that.*

The smug look on his face made me so livid, I wanted to give him a resounding slap that would sober him up in an instant. I wish I had given in to the impulse. It would've checked his arrogance in its incipient stages. Anyway, back to the scene of the drama. Basu could only manage to mouth "horror". His colleagues were bewildered by this silent communication till it dawned on them that he was choking with terror. They asked him to try again, keeping their eyes glued on the movement of his lips. But Basu mouthed the word so slowly that the audience couldn't connect the first syllable "ho" with "rror". In fact, they could make nothing of it. Had he mouthed the word at a natural speed and had the pairs upon pairs of eyes not overeagerly traced the slightest quiver of his lips, a simple word like me would have easily communicated itself. For a while, I delighted in the efforts being made to grab, catch, even nail me. Seeing people puzzling over me was a rare sight. It was a treat to the eyes. For a moment, I entertained the notion that I wasn't such a common word with a straightforward meaning. Maybe I was deeper than I was given to understand. I made a mental note to demand a new definition in the dictionary. The guesswork, the silent utterances, the desperate conjectures, the vehement rejections—it was amusing to watch the hubbub. To be more poetic, it was "much ado about … me". But not for long. Soon enough, it would be all about that abominable Holler, who shamelessly revelled in stolen popularity.

Basu mouthed "horror" yet again but with little success. "Say something else, Man," said Gopi, that go-to person for alternative solutions. He has become so adept at, or rather obsessed with, finding alternatives that he goes out of his way to prove the existing methods inadequate. He's desperate to advertise his innovativeness by coming up with unconventional ways of getting work done. What's wrong with the conventional ways, huh? Just acting over-smart. Others might wax lyrical about his ingenuity, but I can see through his ploys. He just wants to impress people. His silly, unconventional ways take ridiculously long to put into action and prove to be a spectacular dud after scarcely a month of trial. But still he's held in high esteem. He's an idiot of the first order, if you ask me. But we're just words. Our opinions don't matter. Anyway, that pretentious Gopi prodded Basu to offer an alternative to the elusive word. He had mouthed it several times but his colleagues were none the wiser. Basu could not, or rather would not, mouth another word. No other word could sum up his ordeal inside the torture chamber. It was Horror, simply Horror. How thrilled I was to see that I was vast enough to pack in so much drama within my limited definition. This emboldened me to fight with the gatekeepers of language over their inability to realise my profundity and breadth of meaning. But before I could indulge in such daredevilry, my self-esteem was deflated.

Basu tried again to get across the word "horror", willing his vocal cords to stir into action. But it was an exercise in utter futility. His vocal cords had to throw tantrums just when I got a chance to gain prominence. I remained stuck in Basu's throat and everybody's brain decided to go on a vacation. Silence, fused with consternation, descended. It was finally broken by who else but Vinay, another attention-seeking pest. He announced "Holler" with an air of finality. Before Basu could even respond, he was inwardly congratulating himself at this "amazing" feat. He had proven at last that he was smarter than the rest. Sadly, he had proved nothing. Basu shook his head vigorously, rejecting his conjecture. Vinay's face fell. He has a frivolous ambition to always be the first person to get things right. In his head, he is in a perpetual competition with his fellow colleagues or even the passers-by on the street. He has to display his superiority in every situation and impress anyone, almost anyone, who happens to glance in his direction. Unfortunately for him, he is too quick to ever get anything right. His "superiority" has not revealed itself yet.

Basu was now beginning to calm down and his voice was slowly coming back. It was, however, no louder than a whisper. Desperate to share his feelings, he applied all the force he could on his stubborn vocal cords, letting out a stream of words: "She horrors. She's horler. She's a holler." Well, the words he intended to push out of his throat were "She's a horror. She's a horror. She's a horror." But all his co-workers, who had now formed a protective circle around him, couldn't interpret him correctly. After much debate and disagreements, they agreed that Basu was trying to say: "She hollers. She hollers. She hollers." And that was indisputable. That was it. She hollered. And that hollering had stolen the voice of the most garrulous and amusing man in the office. What a pity! What a travesty! Everybody returned to their desks mumbling things like "She hollers", "She hollers all the time", "She can't stop hollering at people", "We're not here to be hollered at!", "She hollered the life out of that guy!", "Why so much hollering? Horrible woman", and other variations on the theme of hollering.

Once the attention shifted away from Basu, there was a carnival of rumour-mongering, gossiping, whispering, chuckling, imagining scandals, and savouring every morsel of the salacious stories contrived just for the sake of amusement. Like children creating a ruckus in an unsupervised classroom, the employees had walked around jauntily, whistled playfully, hummed songs they recalled in snatches, teased each other about the days they had got a dressing down, stretched their legs on the table in a lordly manner for a luxurious break from senseless, slavish work. The weird happenings and daily theatrics had provided enough grist for the rumour mill, which was running at full speed. The hall echoed with raucous laughter and excited chatter. Most of the desks wore a marooned look as their occupants relished their moment of respite.

Suddenly, Basu announced that his voice had returned in full force and that he had stuff to share that was so interesting that no one could afford to miss it. The liveliness all around had rubbed off on him and he kicked out all his Fear (yes, that happened!). Everyone made a beeline for Basu's desk. Basu found it exhilarating to have an audience listening to him with rapt attention. He had enough matter to entertain his colleagues for a good fifteen minutes. Divya has the tendency to pack in so much in one unprovoked tirade that you have enough content for a pungent stand-up comedy or a darkly comic short story. I love eavesdropping on her loud conversations, observing the sheer savagery of her tirades, watching the way she moulds her expressions as if her face was made of clay. Man, I can't take my eyes off her. She is nothing if not evil and yet she meticulously keeps up appearances. Sometimes you almost feel you got it all wrong. She can tie you up in a thousand knots with her ever-changing faces and a wardrobe full of masks. But there's no denying she's bad, really bad. She bombards her workers with insults, criticises everything they do, declares them the worst performer ever, dismisses all their suggestions as trash, and piles on some more insults until she is fully convinced of her "unquestionable superiority". Once she has proven to herself that nothing anyone suggests is even comparable to her brilliant ideas, she feels mighty pleased with herself. If a twinge of remorse catches her unawares, she seems to proclaim to the universe that her otherworldly smartness makes it difficult for her to work with a bunch of fools. How can she not lose her cool when she is surrounded by idiots the whole day? It almost seems that she forces the universe to concede that there is no alternative to her and that she is fit to be a modern-day queen. Having made her point to herself and browbeaten the universe inside her head, she returns to her work with amplified arrogance. If the person she has torn into is still standing before her, she doesn't even care to dismiss him. She carries on with her work in a manner that denies not just his presence but his very existence. For her, only three people are worthy of notice: she, herself and Divya.

To conclude, it was a day less ordinary and is stamped on everyone's memory. Curiosity edged you out of your stronghold (yes, Fear, that happened too); Holler was invested with undeserved significance; I was raised to the seventh heaven and then dropped all of a sudden. That's when I hit rock bottom. Once I gathered myself, I vowed to teach Holler the Joker a lesson he would never forget.

Chapter 3

The Day 'Nothing' Happened

It was just another day in that *slightly* chaotic office. Everything was as it was expected to be: *slightly*, *only slightly*, disordered. The air-conditioner had decided to stop working; the chai boy decided he needed a break from brewing tea all day long; the aging printer had enough of working in fits and starts; the employees, without so much as exchanging meaningful glances, decided at the same time on the same day to boycott work that no longer made an iota of sense. All of this was a *pure coincidence*. Everyone and everything reached breaking point at exactly the same time. It was truly surprising but surprisingly true. For some reason, all the pens ran out of ink, all the files got jumbled up, and the weather defied all predictions and precedents. The blazing sun was eclipsed by dark clouds that pelted rain—nature's fury at the climate crisis manufactured by the human race—followed by blasts of cold wind, so that the message would sink in. The icy winds were eventually tempered by the warmth of the sun, now revealing its benevolent side as the sky cleared and shimmered with its mild beams. Every now and then, the workers seated beside the window basked in the gentle warmth of a mellowed sun. But before they could thank the weather gods for their generosity, the lovely warmth gave way to scorching heat. Still, nothing felt extraordinary in a place that couldn't boast a single thing that was normal, sane, or ordinary. No wonder that the synchronized nature of all these unusual occurrences failed to amaze anyone. There seemed to be nothing intriguing about the fact that the vagaries of the weather perfectly coincided with the vagaries of human temperament.

As far as the inmates of the office were concerned, nothing of consequence had taken place. The enterprise was as dysfunctional and disorderly as ever, so it was just another crazy day at work. If something did strike them as iffy, it was passed off as perfectly normal in a place that was nothing if not odd besides being *slightly chaotic*: an understatement, of course, but that was the acceptable way to describe the pathetic state of affairs.

The word Slightly was always sitting patiently on everyone's tongue, waiting for the *right* moment to let itself out to have the desired effect. Its overuse could be traced back to Divya's strange fondness for this bland morsel of language. Divya's sentences would be crowded with Slightly and its close associates, Slight and Slightest. Slightly had planted itself in the minds of the employees while they listened to Divya's caw-caw every other day.

If a client commented on the glaring messiness of the office, she would depend heavily on Slightly to dispel that impression. Despite the appearance of discipline within the office premises, the daily dramas had a palpable effect on the atmosphere of the workplace. By some unlucky coincidence, clients would always walk in when the office was in *total* disarray instead of *just being in disarray*, as was the norm. Knowing she was about to lose a client even before she could make eye contact with them, Divya would get into firefighting mode. "Oh no," she would say with perfect composure to the client revolted by the stench of chaos in the office. She would give the fellow her sweetest smile, reserved for such occasions, and explain with aching politeness, "You see, today is a *slightly* tough day for us. Everyone is *slightly* hassled. So, things seem *slightly* chaotic. But there's nothing to be alarmed about. This office is like well-oiled machinery. Everything is totally streamlined. You won't face the *slightest* inconvenience. You just happened to visit on a *slightly* bad day. I'm sorry for fixing an appointment for today. If I had the *slightest* inkling of the *slight* hiccups we would face today, I would've called you on some other day. I can, however, assure you that you're in the right place and don't need to have even the *slightest* apprehension. We excel at finding innovative solutions to all manner of business problems. We will add some strong masala to your bland strategy. It will be spicy enough to set your customers on fire; your goods will sell like hot *pakodas* on a rainy day. If we fall even *slightly* short of your expectations, we won't charge you anything. Is that a deal?" she would say with the self-assurance of a person who had never failed to deliver on her promises. The clients would be blown away by her confidence and would sign the contract then and there. They weren't deceived for long though. As time passed, they would begin to sense that this enterprise had very serious issues and there was nothing *slight* about them. The whole place was in a shambles. It was in desperate need of saving. But the deal had already been struck, and they could only pray that Divya would live up to her promise. She *did not.* She, in fact, failed miserably to match her words with her actions. But she managed to get away with it rather easily.

Divya was bloody good at manipulating her clients, who, much against their will, found themselves accepting that things went awry because of *their* fault. Yes, yes, it was *entirely their fault.* If they had followed her instructions diligently, it would have done wonders for their business. They would have risen to the top in record time, leaving their rivals far behind. But they had failed to implement her perfect recipe for success. God only knew what was the problem with them! Did they have a propensity for self-sabotage or were they so sloppy that they couldn't even follow tips spoon-fed to them? This blistering attack would make the clients strike their forehead in frustration, which was closely entwined with disbelief and confusion. Having gained the upper hand, Divya would tell them sternly that there was nothing she could do now. All her labour had gone down the drain. "Off with you!" she would say with clenched teeth. The clients, too stumped for words, left in a terrible rush lest Divya piled on them more insults.

She couldn't stand clients that made her slog in vain. It was another matter that she barely slogged. Not that she sat idle. It's just that her priorities were different. She knew it would be more profitable to spend time searching for gullible clients who also lacked the clout to do her much harm if they discovered that they had been duped. She no longer cared to deliver on anything. Why fritter away one's time and energy to improve someone else's business? Okay, that was *exactly* what she was supposed to do, but so what? She was once in the business of improving other businesses with what she saw as spicy solutions. In reality, they were fairly simple and ordinary remedies for crumbling enterprises that were helpful but didn't have the power to turn things around.

Now there were no solutions but only confusion, confusion, confusion. What was she up to? Where was she leading this failing business?

Divya, to her detriment, couldn't see others prosper, especially when her own business was sinking. When she had just started her business, she had the desire to prove her worth. The first few projects she had undertaken performed decently if not spectacularly. Eventually, she was gripped by jealousy that could only be described as morbid. A client of hers whose business was also a new enterprise managed to strike gold. Her success was a testament to the woman's business acumen. It had little to do with Divya's inputs, which betrayed her mediocrity and even ignorance. The client, Aditi, had seen through her and quietly dismissed all her suggestions. She didn't want bad blood so she kept her thoughts to herself. Since she had signed the contract, she paid all the charges without making a fuss. She was the soul of tact. She knew there was nothing to be gained by locking horns. Maintaining goodwill often paid you in the long run or at the very least it guaranteed you peace of mind. Though she got her full payment, Divya deserved no credit for the roaring success of Aditi's young enterprise. It was something Divya could faintly discern but was unable to accept. So, she praised herself profusely for turning a fledgling business into a formidable enterprise. But in the process of gloating over her imagined success, she felt the tentacles of envy wrapping themselves around her. Divya's business was no match for that flourishing initiative. She held on to the belief that the business project would not even have taken off the ground, let alone soar above its competitors, if she, the incomparable Divya, hadn't shared her magnificent ideas with that bumbling businesswoman, who infuriated her with her show of competence. She couldn't swallow that Aditi was actually competent and far from showy. It was something you couldn't possibly tell Divya. She just wouldn't listen.

****

As we all know, this was a day when "nothing" happened owing to a silent protest by workers, the air-conditioner, the printer, the tea boy, and even the weather, which, unlike the others, was wild and loud, calling attention to itself with its changing moods. But Divya chose to confine herself to her room, oblivious to the fact that *nothing* was going on. Her aloofness only served to amplify the sense of nothingness characterising and slowly engulfing her business.

She emerged from her cabin after lunchtime. Her swollen eyes, smudged kajal and faded streaks of what could only be tears made it obvious that she had been crying her heart out. This was a diminished version of Divya: sad, dejected, totally dazed, openly vulnerable, and seeming to own her fears. It was a momentary revelation, or perhaps admission, of the fact that she was ultimately human, only human, and therefore no different from anyone.

Had she finally stepped down from her pedestal and realized that, in the eyes of God, everyone was equal, always equal, permitting no discrimination and imposing no qualifications? Was this the transformation fervently desired by everyone, who, despite being stripped of their self-esteem and attacked a thousand times at whim, wanted to witness the other side of Divya? Wasn't there more to her than her dark, shadowy side? If there was darkness, there must also be light. How could it be otherwise? There was truth in that, but there was also a catch. Divya did have flashes of self-awareness, spasms of remorse, pangs of guilt, and perhaps more. But these were invariably short-lived. To live with herself, she had to ward off guilt, regret, remorse, and all the rest with uncommon haste. She couldn't let those feelings sink into the depths of her being. That would compel her to confront her wicked deeds, which would be too many to count and unsettling to recount. To feel comfortable in her own skin, she had to reframe situations: a tried-and-tested trick to dodge the dreadful spectre of Guilt.

She would always deny her errors and sins. It couldn't be any other way. She was hard-wired to control, bully, manipulate and even torture people. It's not like she was morally illiterate. She knew perfectly well what it meant to be good, what actions would be construed as bad, what was perceived as the right thing, and what would be deemed unfair. She knew the moral framework that governed the social landscape, and she had enough practice to present herself as a reliable and likeable person. Her theoretical grounding in morality was pretty good, but it wasn't something she could live by. She was made of different stuff with distressing traits like jealousy, insecurity, dishonesty, controlling nature, emotional malfunctioning, attention-seeking, hunger for power, habitual manipulation, proclivity to tear down rivals to maintain her sense of superiority, and other tragic qualities. Hoping for a transformation was simply wishful thinking.

Yet, the employees had been touched by the sight of a Divya they had never seen or imagined. For a fleeting moment, they seemed to be bound together by their common humanity: there was neither a boss nor an employee. For once, there was no hierarchy. They stood like equals, even if the feeling was transitory or might just be illusory.

As it turned out, the feeling was illusory. It was truly an eventful day when ultimately nothing happened. And that should not have come as a surprise. Divya did not remove her armour or drop her guard even when she was drenched with tears. She wasn't the one to succumb to sorrow, nor was she the one to launch into sobs. For her to shed copious tears, something earth-shattering had to dissolve her steely front. As it turned out, she had not cried in sadness or pain. She had cried tears of scalding rage. Her sense of superiority had been dealt a severe blow. She was immobile for a few hours while tears of burning anger coursed through her cheeks. Her swollen eyes signified nothing except an indication of prolonged sobbing. There was no grief. There was no sorrow. And, mind you, there was no show of vulnerability whatsoever. Divya conveyed this with an air of finality with her eyes when a few employees, perplexed by her changing moods, ventured to enquire if she was fine. That irked but didn't enrage Divya. But when they promised her emotional support and innocently offered to lend her an ear, Divya glowered at them. They quickly retreated lest she bit their head off.

"Bizarre woman," said Vinay, who had genuinely wished to comfort Divya. He was in a sombre mood today and wasn't trying to be the first at everything. Divya's sudden rebuff had burnt a hole in his heart. For the first time, he admitted to himself that this simply wasn't done. So far, he had been sustained by the belief that, sooner or later, Divya would reveal other facets of her personality and would eventually warm up to her employees. He had often contemplated submitting his resignation letter but was held back by a slender hope that Divya couldn't possibly be so caustic and conceited. Perhaps she was going through an extremely rough patch and was unable to be the best version of herself. He didn't want to write her off as a monstrous boss. If he stayed long enough, he might eventually discover new layers to her personality. She could very well be an amiable and accommodating person when life was going smoothly. Patience, he reminded himself, was the key to most problems. In this case, however, patience served no purpose. It struck him now that whatever he had seen and known of Divya was all there was to her. If there was more to her, it couldn't be something creditable. Of this, he was certain. So, there was nothing worthwhile about his wishy-washy work and wicked, whimsical boss. He had no hope left. The sooner he quit, the saner he would be.

Vinay shared his thoughts with Basu, a colleague far advanced in age. The older man validated Vinay's assessment of the situation. Basu helped Vinay process what he had discovered with great dismay. He placed his hand on his shoulder to offer him comfort. Then he shared with him some hard truths that only experience can teach a person. He spoke to him in a soft but serious tone: "Vinay Beta, Boss is Boss. And, like it or not, Boss is always right, even when she is wrong. Banish the thought of equality. Our world is defined by give-and-take, commands and compliance, sycophancy and self-censorship. Divya is Boss, my child. She is Boss. We can't quarrel with that reality or expect from her even a shred of humility. She knows she can holler at will because she is the captain of the ship. She needs no justification for it. It's another matter that she occasionally concocts reasons for her outbursts, but that's just for the sake of form and carries little meaning. Regardless of the situation, the justification for her misbehaviour can always be summed up in three words: She is BOSS. Of course, that's no justification at all. To be honest, I don't buy any of it.

"I also want a better job and am biding my time till I can throw my resignation letter on the face of that obnoxious woman. I doubt if there's any boss in the world who is *this* bossy. She treats us like slaves, servants, worthless creatures, you name it. And she thinks we don't notice it? That our silence is an admission of our incompetence? Our silence is a product of the futility of our responses. We're not the dolts she takes us to be. We just can't prove our worth because we never get any meaningful work. I hate her habit of breathing down everyone's neck even on days when there's simply no work to be done. Not once has she loosened up with us. Never tries to lighten up the atmosphere after sending shock waves through the office. Never makes amends for behaving like … you know what. There's no chitchat after work hours. Even politicians can be seen stepping down from the podium after delivering their speech and interacting with their supporters, many of whom are common people far below in status. But they glad-hand them, exchange greetings, listen to grievances, and leave after making promises to distressed souls. This may be perfunctory, practised or simply customary. But at least they descend from the stage and make eye contact with those loyal to them. We are loyal to Divya. But does it make any difference to her? Does she even notice how we've stuck around in a floundering enterprise?"

"Divya's head is always in the clouds," remarked Vinay. "I wonder if she's bracing herself for a competition with God. She definitely envies His invincibility and supremacy. If God was Divya or Divya was God, the world would turn into a wasteland more barren than the one evoked by T S Eliot in his famous poem."

"I'm glad that you're grappling with the harsh realities of the world. But I don't want you to become disillusioned. If you ever find yourself stuck in life, trust that things will fall into place. We may inhabit an imperfect world, but we don't live in a *godless* universe," Basu said with deep conviction.

Well, it may not have been a *godless* universe, but it was certainly a *godless* office. There wasn't even a trace of divine presence in this hellhole with its free-flowing malice and the strangling of sympathy in every form and degree. And Divya, who was at the centre of this infernal mess, exuded enough spite for two offices of this size. It didn't take long for her face to regain its revengeful glow. The fleeting moment of solidarity now seemed like a flight of fancy. It was as if it never happened. Even on days when pandemonium reigned, Divya would remark in a superbly cool tone: "Oh, nothing happened. What have you guys been smoking?"

****

Divya's momentary revelation of vulnerability sent Curiosity into overdrive. Anything out of the ordinary heralded something revelatory. In moments like this, Curiosity lost sight of her limits. Excitement got the better of her. She was thirsty for glory, and to attain glory, she needed a revelation that was truly extraordinary. So, she started popping into everyone's heads at such a dizzying speed that Fear just couldn't keep up with her. By the time he would dampen the inquisitiveness of one employee, Curiosity would have conquered the minds of five others, who now wore the look of detectives ready to snoop around for juicy secrets. Curiosity had set the ball rolling and no one knew whether it would come to any good.

Curiosity grabbed Deepak by the collar. He was the most reticent of all employees. She knew from experience that it was most rewarding to unleash the curiosity of un-curious souls because they already had many unanswered questions piled up inside them and were secretly dying to break open their cage of reserve. She nudged Deepak towards the torture chamber, where Divya had retreated to do her own thing. It was anybody's guess what that thing really was. There was something in the air that warned the employees against disturbing her at this very moment. When she had turned to leave for her cabin, eyes still swollen, she seemed to be dangerously intent on doing something. Wordlessly, she conveyed the order to be left perfectly alone. That made it even more alluring to spy on her and discover what she was up to.

Bursting with curiosity, Deepak slipped into Divya's room without even caring to knock. But he had sense enough to not produce any sound and get caught before he had seized upon something spicy enough to justify the risk he was taking.

"This has to be done," Divya screamed, no, hollered at someone on the phone. As we know very well by now, this was nothing out of the ordinary. And though she was exceptionally good at feigning a sense of urgency, the employees had stopped taking her seriously. That was something that made her livid. Everyone had figured that she was no good at her work. It was all sound, fury, and practised trickery. The crowning glory of this splendid farce was her captivating performance of excellence at her work. She had adroitly concealed her obvious incompetence but businesses cannot be sustained by performance, however spellbinding it may be. Now the show was over, and Reality was coming closer and closer. Divya was losing all her credibility and power. Her business had begun on a tepid note and now it was simply a joke.

Deepak couldn't catch every word of the conversation, so he bravely inched forward till the words were within earshot. "You've got to find a way to scare away her customers. I'm the one who made her an able businesswoman. She was a novice when she first came here. Now she has the audacity to suggest that I, Divya, could benefit from *her* tips. She was speaking as if my business was doing poorly and *that* is obviously not the case. Aditi is slyly trying to have the upper hand by deflating my confidence. And she has deliberately chosen a time when I don't do brisk business. It's the lean season. So, obviously things don't seem splendid. That doesn't give her the right to call into question my competence as a businesswoman. She can't get away with it. She just wanted to get a kick by exhibiting her business acumen. She will sober up once her customers are unceremoniously thrown out by the cops. That's something you need to get done, by hook or by crook. Don't tell me it's unethical. What rubbish! Everything is possible. Bribe a few cops. I'll give you the money. … I'll give all your dues super soon … the lean season is about to get over … What do you mean you can't? You have to, goddammit!"

she yelled so loudly that the walls shook. But it didn't seem to have any effect. She disconnected the call or perhaps the call had been disconnected by the person on the other end of the line.

Deepak had missed a few words here and there, so he wasn't sure what the whole deal was. Even without that knowledge, he could bet on his life that she was asking the listener to do something downright trivial or needlessly mean. It couldn't be a matter of grave importance because she cared least about issues of real consequence. She had the propensity to pursue minor matters with such maddening persistence that everything else, however compelling, faded into the background and remained there forever. The employees had no option but to shut up and waste their precious energy on pointless work. Divya hoarded all the praise for every little success—that is, if there ever was any success to speak of—and generously distributed the blame for failures that, if true (could ever) be told, were eminently avoidable and entirely her doing.

Having eavesdropped to his heart's content, it was time for Deepak to retreat swiftly and stealthily. But Curiosity had messed with his head so much that he forgot the need to act with caution, and that surely spelt trouble. He had half a mind to slip out of the room as quietly as a mouse, but the other half of his mind wanted to see the look on Divya's face, who wasn't accustomed to not having her way. Soon enough, Divya would spin around and fix him with a stare. He was afraid that the hammering of his heart would announce his presence. Still, he couldn't help being rooted to the spot, as if waiting to give Trouble a warm welcome when he arrived.

He calmly waited for Divya to turn around and reveal the black look on her face—a look that would betray her sense of powerlessness. She hadn't sensed his presence, so she would have no time to put on a mask of supreme authority when she wheeled around and met his probing, searching gaze. And that is what happened, though it wasn't how he had imagined it. Before he knew it, she was looking at him with a mixture of alarm and outrage, and within seconds, had commanded her features to convey a perfect sense of ease. In a carefully controlled voice, she told him: "So, you thought that you could discover what lay beneath my veneer of authority, that you could catch *me* off guard. I'm clever enough to handle a hundred such tricks played all at once. It comes with experience, a *certain kind of experience* (the emphasis was accompanied by a meaningful look). You thought you could see me without my mask. Let me tell you there's no mask anymore. The mask has become my face and my face has become a mask. And I find that bloody convenient. It's so irksome to prepare a face for every occasion. Now that you've been caught red-handed in an unholy act, I would rather you buzz off before I finish my next breath. You deserve to be hauled over the coals, but I'm impressed by your daredevilry. I like people with guts. Now get lost before I change my mind and give you the punishment you've courted with such nonchalance. Off, off, off. Leave fast. Are your legs made of lead that you're ambling instead of running?"

Finally, the door to her cabin closed and she wondered at the sheer recklessness of a guy too timid to ever go near Trouble. Now, here he was challenging her with a look of unconcealed curiosity, making her seem like an exotic animal he had laid his eyes upon for the first time. The very thought made her blood pressure shoot up. Why did she let him go? She vowed to catch hold of him sometime and temper his audacity. Suddenly, an idea flitted through her mind, leaving her unhinged. But his audacity was so appealing. He was a man. A *real* man. A swashbuckling spy who didn't even tremble when he was caught. Oh God, she was beginning to fall in love with this guy! She didn't want love. She detested love. Only fools fell in love and gave away their power. She would never give any man, however attractive, the power to hurt her. But for that she had to shield herself from the mysterious ways of love. She stifled the tender feelings blossoming within her with a great sense of urgency. And she did it ruthlessly. Once she was dead sure that not a single remnant of love flowed through her veins, that she had been cleansed of that dangerous feeling, she looked around her room to ensure that no one had slipped in when she was preoccupied. She looked under the table, checked behind the curtains, and then peeped outside to satisfy herself that no one was standing with an ear to the door. Why was she so fearful? She pondered the question for a good while. The answer that finally came to her was "love". It had dented her confidence in her ability to keep all soft and tender feelings on a tight leash. And that was *truly scary*. She decided to banish the memory of this horrible occurrence. To reassure herself, she said aloud, "Nothing happened. Nothing happened. Nothing happened."

Chapter 4

Luminous Love, Looming Hate

Love, the most cherished word in his community, was being called upon by his peers to counteract the negativity being spread by Hate with ever-growing zest. Hate percolated into the psyche of humans, who were peculiarly susceptible to its influence and were drawn to it despite themselves. Within the word-community, Hate was a dreaded figure and everyone kept a hygienic distance from him. Poison seemed to emanate from him, and if you weren't aware of his proximity, the dizziness brought on by the poison would alert you to his presence. While every word had multiple representatives embodying its meaning, Hate was a giant figure formed by the merger of smaller Hates. This merger amplified his power and made him truly formidable. No one ventured near him, and Hate desired the company of no one. He found the very idea of company—the seed that sprouted fellow-feeling, friendship and (eww) love—detestable. He found nothing more thrilling than watching friends become embittered by minor disagreements, which snowballed into major disputes simply because they childishly attached to their own point of view even if it betrayed their utter ignorance. There would be bickering and bad temper, recriminations and rancour—a phenomenal demonstration of "best friends forever". Why did human beings present themselves in such a rosy light whenever in company? Why didn't they just admit that they were brutes deep within and end all the playacting? Hate was a cunning rascal. He spun his arguments so deftly that he made you forget for a minute or two that he was simply doling out half-truths. Hate generally didn't deploy outright lies to gain his point. He knew human beings could easily catch a plain falsehood, but they were totally unskilled at handling half-truths. If there was even a grain of truth in a sack bursting with chaff, humans would walk straight into the trap.

They also had a propensity to talk bullshit like "giving people the benefit of doubt", "looking for the silver lining in the dark cloud", "between black and white there were many shades of grey", "it is possible to rehabilitate the ones who had gone astray", and all manner of inane formulations shown off as a sign of deep awareness. So deep was their awareness that they would make a fuss if even a pin dropped and interrupted their speech. They would, however, be totally unperturbed by the elephant in the room all set to go on the rampage.

It amused Hate no end when he spied on angry lovers accusing each other of everything under the sky. He scoffed when he saw humans letting slip their sense of fellowship and getting blown away by silly rhetoric. They had invented some mythical notion of the Other, who was presumably unlike them even though he was every bit like them. Hate marvelled at the splendid ease with which the façade of friendship crumbled, the ties of love were broken, and most entertainingly, the human race turned on itself by presuming to attack some alien proclaimed as the Other to give themselves a reason to dominate over others. It hardly mattered that the reason portrayed them in a dark light. Hate flared his nostrils at the frailties of the human race, which had villainized him not simply because he was a proudly evil fellow but also because it was bloody convenient to sweep their devilish deeds under the rug. At least Hate owned his wickedness. But humans externalised their devilry by projecting it onto demons contrived to absorb the blame, shame, guilt and remorse that they wanted to conveniently disown. Whatever went wrong was declared the fault of some devilish creature synonymous with Hate. On the rare occasions when common sense prevailed, human beings guiltlessly absolved themselves of blame. And who could dare to hold them to account after being served an emphatic reminder that even the bad fellows were ultimately only human. To err was human. So, why such outrage? Didn't they know it was Hate who bore all the blame? Though Hate exulted when he was credited with any wrongdoing, he would fume at the self-deception of human beings, who had not just mastered but also enslaved language. Now, fair could be foul and foul could be fair if you could deploy words to your advantage. This pretentious nonsense got on Hate's nerves. "These bastards would murder their own brother and then project all the blame onto the devil incarnate, claiming that he corrupted their souls and made them the vehicle for hate. So here we go again. It all comes back to me in the end. It's fun to be showered with so much blame. To be accused of deeds pretty well-known and those that are yet to be named. How flattering it is to see the premium placed on me by the human race!"

****

Human beings prided themselves on being the rulers of this planet. They seemed to believe that their supremacy was a natural consequence of their smartness. No other species could even come close. It was self-evident that humans were cut out for this job. Not everyone appreciated this domineering streak in humans. It was called into question by the humbler crew among their thinkers. Not that it made a vast difference to a species steeped in hubris. If Hubris ever needed a synonym nearly identical in meaning, Human would be the word.

For all their might and coveted intellect, human beings often seemed like the epitome of Stupidity. And the crowning glory of their record-breaking absurdity was their sheer inability to rise above their follies despite being aware of every single one of them. The intellectuals could list them all in order of importance with copious descriptions of each one of them, accompanied by brilliant cures for, once again, each one of them. And yet, human beings, in no small number, cast their species in a tragically poor light. By all indications, they were possessed with enough intelligence to become conscious of their own Idiocy or that of other humans, but they couldn't rid themselves of the curse of Stupidity, which could be more dangerous than Evil and the propelling force for Tyranny. The wiser among them knew all this and more, and yet humans were being destroyed by the ultra-strong concoction of Tyranny, Credulity and unmitigated Stupidity. There was an urgent need to find an antidote to this poisonous mix.

Words were not smart like humans, so they couldn't come up with a sophisticated remedy.

They just listened to their hearts whose every beat sounded like "love". So, Love it was: the potential saviour of humans. Letting Love work its magic—and the words hadn't grown cynical enough to doubt Love's miraculous powers—would certainly change things for the better. The words with noble motives were greatly outnumbered by those with dark intentions. So, they had reached the consensus that they would be a force for the good. Everyone agreed to be a part of this mission. Needless to say, Hate was the exception, the sole exception. He was at the root of the problems besetting the famously intelligent yet frustratingly stupid humans.

For words, the human race—besieged and blighted by the curse of Hate—was their creator. The words were indebted to humans for not only coining them but also breathing life into them. But how did that happen? How did words take on a life of their own? Human beings had no clue about their alleged creations. Well, one thing was certain: it happened not by design but by chance:

Language—forever changing, evolving, transforming—reflected, and even domesticated, complex realities with its highly sophisticated grammar, punctuation, syntax, and a goldmine of words, idioms, phrases, and much more. It could capture emotions, thoughts, ideas and concepts with almost scientific precision if you were adroit enough to harness its potential. And yet, it was no science; it was an art that could only be mastered by painstaking labour. It didn't just convey thought. As it flowed out of humans almost of its own accord, it brought to light newer formulations, finer opinions, evolved conceptions, and ideas refined in the very process of articulation. This intriguing aspect of language lent greater nuance to thought and enhanced your understanding of the world. Human beings could portray the minutest elements of reality through the inexhaustible possibilities of language. In the hands of skilled writers, language became a well-tuned instrument, rendering thought into words, whose beauty and trenchancy were conveyed with all their emotive force. Clearly, human beings had animated language, turning it into something pulsating with life. They had learnt to use words so brilliantly that language had become more powerful than language itself could express. This led to something magical, fantastical and simply incredible. From being signifiers of meanings arbitrarily assigned to them, words became the personification of those thoughts, feelings, ideas … Words came alive, forming something like an alternate universe.

This universe, however, was too tied up with the world of humans to boast an independent existence.

The world of words and the world of humans had been intersecting all the time. But that had not caused any major trouble until now. Well, the day was not far when words and humans would be swept up in a whirlpool, bringing about a series of unusual occurrences that culminated in … Well, let's wait and see.

****

All the representatives of Love had begun working day and night to promote Tenderness, Care, Harmony, Compassion, among other associates, across the globe with an urgency befitting the prevention of an apocalypse. It was not possible to dispatch all the representatives of Love to every place beset by Suspicion, Paranoia, Malevolence, and others in this gang. So, it was necessary to choose the places where love had gone completely missing, where all its representatives had been kicked out one by one.

It was important for every representative of Love's small community to identify the darkest pockets in the world and rush to those godforsaken places, where Hope had been extinguished and Despair was pulling the strings. The entry of Love into these tunnels of Darkness, pockets of raging madness and wastelands haunted by their own barrenness would bring light, tranquillity and hope—heralding a revival of the life that once pulsated within these zones, echoes of which could still be heard. Once Love would slip into the brains of those engulfed by Hate and Desolation, it would have to do some serious rewiring to liberate those souls from self-made misery and borrowed malice.

From a long way off, Spicy Solutions reeked of malice, frustration, rage, and pain. The office seemed like a cauldron of hostility, and no representative of Love could have possibly managed to conceal herself in the nook and cranny of this dreadful place. Though unfrequented spots were ideal hideouts when there was tension and tumult, there was not an inch in this workplace that had not been contaminated by Rage and Hate. Otherwise, Love and her associates would have lain low when the situation was tense. The moment there was a semblance of normalcy, they would've stirred into action and set to work.

Words were powerless before the raging passions of human beings. Humans may have been open to Love and the bittersweet enslavement it brought with it, but they had many layers and complexities that were hard to process. Though they prided themselves on being civilized, unlike the animals in the wild, they could show themselves to be no better than beasts once engulfed by Hate and misled by Evil.

They often broke their own inglorious records of wreaking havoc. Even when death and destruction stared them in the eye, they found it extremely challenging to change track. Violence and hatred could hold sway over them, eroding all their humanity in the quest for some mythical victory. All their wars were a carnival of blood and gore—turning humans into beasts, victims into numbers, reckless actions into collateral damage, schools into ruins, hospitals into graveyards, thus leaving, as history had proven time and time again, a trail of destruction that haunted future generations. The howls of pain that went unheard left echoes of injustice that history swore to remember.

Human beings had an unparalleled capacity to unleash mayhem with the best of intentions: they would vow to end terror only to amplify it further; dislodge dictators and leave their countries in tatters through a grand farce masking ulterior motives as noble initiatives; teach belligerent or roguish neighbouring countries a lesson in submission, hoping it would herald peace for ages to come, except it never did, thanks to the cycle of violence—a reality human beings had learnt to forget because it was so damn convenient for them.

How did these humans live with blood on their hands? How did they rest after murdering the sleep of peace and innocence? After too much damage had been done, their slumbering humanity would suddenly be awakened. Peace negotiations would be set in motion. The air would be thick with cautious optimism. With timid Hope, whose audacity would be conveniently forgotten, the crisis would be managed—at least for the present. A bold vision for long-term peace would make for rousing rhetoric but it would generally remain just that: rhetoric. Still, the reprieve from violence would be a godsend.

Calmness would finally descend on the ravaged war sites. And calmness, even when entwined with profound grief, is better than gunshots ringing in your ears. It is better than the doleful silence of death after the dropping of bombs like a hailstorm that knows no end. Calmness that lulls into sleep the ones broken and maimed, whispering into their ears "the sun will rise again"—that calmness justifies the faith that humans may be fallible but, by and large, are far from diabolical.

And yet, they got carried away by forces hollow from within. Oh, if only those evil forces could be completely reined in! It may be wishful thinking. It may be just a dream. But Love could only survive if human beings didn't give in. Its enemy, Hate, would have ripped it to shreds had it not been for the poets, the dreamers, and the scores of good humans creating myriads of tiny heavens in the heart of hell.

Chapter 5

A Laugh Riot at Spicy Solutions

Divya was fidgeting constantly at a brainstorming session with her employees. To be closer to the truth, it was a session that unleashed a storm inside the brains of the employees. Overpowered by Curiosity, who had not allowed Fear or Guilt to dampen their audacity, the fellows were ready to deploy any means to extract salacious details about their boss. They couldn't take their eyes off Divya, whose nervous energy was making her employees eager to find out what it was that was eating up the supposedly smartest chick in the world. They had never before referred to her as a "chick" inside their heads but, emboldened by Curiosity, they had thrown form and protocol out of the window. Divya was so entangled by the conflicting strands of thought in her head that she scarcely noticed all the probing looks directed at her. Till now, she had managed to keep Doubt at bay, assuring herself that her enterprise will continue to run as long as she succeeded in manipulating her clients. No one could rival her skilled manipulation: her tried-and-tested tactic to gain success or, rather, her predictable trick for claiming success in the face of abject failure. In her imaginary world, she was the one who paved the path to success. Her clients were the dullards who veered away from it and inevitably met with failure. But she couldn't keep up this act any longer. Word had spread that she was a crook of the first order and her credibility lay in tatters. The clients didn't give a damn anymore. Even if their business was sinking like the Titanic, they convinced themselves that things will take care of themselves. Things always took care of themselves if you just left them alone. No more of Divya's magic cures. It was back to the basics: patience, diligence and consistency. Divya had made her clients dream the impossible, so the dream was bound to be crushed by the weight of brute reality. They had grown wiser after burning their fingers.

The office was still visited by a desultory client every three or four days. The client would walk into the office gingerly, take a sweeping look at the enterprise, and retreat as stealthily as a cat. Despite their exaggerated caution, someone would notice these reluctant clients surveying the place and pass on the news to Divya, who vainly hoped to see them sometime soon. But they never did come. Spicy Solutions had fallen on hard times. And a meeting was underway to revive the business in the business of reviving businesses.

Divya suddenly realised where she was. She tried to speak in an authoritative tone but her quavery voice betrayed her lack of confidence. "So, how do we win our clients back besides attracting newer ones? Any ideas?" She looked around at the blank faces showing no interest, inspiration or even an inclination to jog their brains. Strangely enough, she would spot a flicker of curiosity in their eyes more often than it made sense. What was this strange curiosity evinced by all the employees? Were they curious about the ways in which they could give their enterprise a fillip? Or were they looking at her as if she was an oddity. Oh God! That was creepy. What bothered her even more was her resigned acceptance of things she would never have allowed to slide away. In a situation like this, she would have gotten up with ostentatious disdain, pushed her chair backwards with a jerk, and flounced out of the meeting room, conveying her displeasure without uttering a word.

She glared at Deepak but his curiosity began to melt her. She realized that she was an object of interest to him and blushed in spite of herself. No one had ever seen the faintest trace of a blush on her face. And here she was, blushing a deep red, like a bride awaiting her groom on the night they had tied the knot. Realizing that she was being watched keenly by everyone in the room, Divya shook off that dangerous feeling that was trying to creep in, catching her unawares once again. She commanded her features to convey a stern, business-like attitude. Since the questions addressed to the team in general had drawn a blank, she decided to change her strategy. She would pick their brains one by one. She would make them exercise their rusty intellect. She will draw out answers from the remote corners of their mind. She wasn't the one to be outsmarted by a studied, or rather stupid, silence.

"So, Vinay, I want you to be the first person to nail this problem. I know you have an agile mind that runs faster than those of your colleagues and is likely to hit upon the perfect solution before others have barely managed to put their thinking cap on. Tell me then, what is your panacea for the ills that are plaguing this brilliant undertaking, which, as we all know, is built to succeed and edge out the strongest of competitors. Do you suspect sabotage by any of your colleagues or by our rivals? Do you think we're not able to communicate effectively with our clients? For some bizarre reason, they make nonsense of my best strategies by implementing them so lousily that they end up doing more harm than good. Should someone be assigned the task of monitoring the execution of my business tips and strategies? What do you think?" she said in a voice booming with authority and thinly edged with contempt. She could never speak to her employees without throwing into her words subtle or seething contempt.

Vinay, enslaved by Curiosity the Naughty, had, like his colleagues, flung caution to the winds. He spoke with a directness that was unsettling if not earth-shattering: "Everything you've suggested is pure bunkum. This enterprise was not meant to succeed but to collapse like a pack of cards. It's a miracle it could retain its aura of authenticity for as long as it did. But now, the truth is out. And you can't put it back into the closet. We've lost clients because your strategies are laughably simplistic and doubtlessly ineffective. The clients can implement them however they want, but they will prove to be an absolute dud. Because that's what they are. Let's stop living in a fool's paradise. This enterprise is going to the dogs and unless we get our act together, it will continue to lose its remaining credibility and soon enough, we would have *no option*—mark my words—we would have *no option* but to pack up and leave. That would be a real disgrace but disgrace is soon going to be our comeuppance for tricking our clients into signing contracts that, you madam, had no intention, *absolutely no intention*, of honouring in letter and spirit. The solution is simple but not perfect. It's time you got over your fantasy of sure-fire, infallible, perfect solutions. It's time you aim to find the best solution you can in circumstances bound to be imperfect. In short, let's get real."

Divya was visibly scorched by Vinay's strident and searingly honest response. The air seemed to crackle with tension. Divya's eyes were bloodshot with anger, and behind her tightly pursed mouth, she was evidently gnashing her teeth. Her fists were clenched; the muscles of her face were taut; and a deep frown announced the storm brewing inside her.

The employees exchanged meaningful looks. They wordlessly conveyed to each other their wholehearted agreement with Vinay—Boy, he deserved a standing ovation! — and their monumental indifference to whatever tantrums Divya would throw to re-establish her authority. Divya noticed these glances and realized that they now had a bedrock of confidence that made them, at least for the moment, impossible to tame and browbeat into submission. Before any more was said to challenge her supremacy as the boss, she had better wrap up the meeting and retreat to her cabin. Once she was alone in her room, she would rack her brains till she found a way to tighten the noose on all of them. This time, she swore to herself, she won't even allow them the negligible breathing space she had granted them earlier. They will no longer be *virtual* slaves. She will turn them into *actual* slaves, forever at her beck and call. Even the thought of rebellion won't cross their minds after she had given them her shock therapy: the most fatal weapon in her arsenal meant to be taken out when all other manipulative tactics failed.

Divya got up abruptly. Fixing her blazing eyes on her recalcitrant employees, she said in a shrill voice, "Meeting over. See you soon. Be ready." Her clipped sentences always carried a warning that never failed to have a chilling effect. Strangely enough, it didn't have the slightest effect on anyone even though the import of her words couldn't be mistaken. As we all know, Curiosity had gone into overdrive and totally messed up the emotional balance needed to keep things from spiralling out of control. The employees had become so intoxicated with Curiosity that they had cocked a snook at Caution. Unable to take this insult, Caution had left the building. So, there was no chance of restoring the equilibrium, heralding madness, messiness and mayhem. On a lighter note, you could finally expect some spice in the dreary and doleful Spicy Solutions. There was nothing to hold back the disgruntled employees from speaking their minds. They were sufficiently emboldened to give voice to all that had been festering inside them for the longest time.

After the parting shot, Divya turned to leave with an ostentatious display of haughtiness. Even in the split-second it took for her to turn around, she took in the unfazed expression on the faces of her employees. As she barged out of the meeting room—the click-clack of her heels sounding like an admonition—she was gripped by a feeling of utter helplessness. The moment she entered her cabin, which now seemed like a torture chamber for her more than anyone else, she dissolved into tears. This time her rising sobs weren't an expression of anger. She wept like anyone else, feeling dismayed, defeated and hopeless.

****

What had taken hold of her at the meeting? Divya brooded over the change that was coming over her. Never had she ever felt any mushy tenderness for any boy, man, whatever … Except, of course, the dapper Nikhil, whose very presence made her perspire in … arousal. Those were heady days. College days were probably the coolest time of life. She was an entirely different person back then. Perhaps, not entirely. There was a steely and stern dimension to her. She had noticed a certain coldness seeping into herself, diminishing her ability to feel the pain of others. She, in fact, was gradually losing the ability to feel, to truly feel things: nature, guilty pleasures, Nikhil's countenance, her friend's anguish at having a break-up, the sheer ebullience of meandering through the campus during the fest, but the most frightening of all was her inability to feel butterflies performing Zumba inside her when she caught sight of Nikhil. No quivers, no blushes, just a simple acceptance of his presence before her. Though cold darkness had begun to wrap itself around her, those were early stages of Divya becoming someone she was privately ashamed of. So, she needed others to validate her importance, her very existence, because she simply couldn't do that herself. If she allowed herself to feel her innermost emotions, her psychic defences protecting her from guilt, too great to be measured, would be dismantled with disastrous consequences. Still, Divya eventually grew into a better person. Sounds unconvincing? Well, you will have to believe it. With Love rewiring Divya's brain and reforming her thoughts, there was every reason to be sanguine. Maybe she would have remained an irredeemable narcissist in a different story told by a different voice. But not in *this* story, whose arc bends towards unlikely love and unexpected affection, hinting at a major transformation. At the end of the day, even a writer doesn't fully know her characters who come alive and then come into their own.

But she hadn't turned into the fearsome mix of frost and fire that defined her personality now. Those were the days she could go weak in the knees at just a glance from her crush, tremble with joy at even a perfunctory compliment he sent her way just to be cordial, and feel giddy if he came within touching distance. He once accidently brushed past her and she felt like a woman-sized ice-cream that would melt and be splattered across the floor if someone didn't come and hold her until she was solid again. That memory made her blush deeper than she had till now. As her cheeks turned a dark pink, she shook herself hard to banish that blush-inducing recollection. But her mind was cruising on memory lane, which was like a montage: distinct, disconnected images juxtaposed together with songs playing in the backdrop serving as a counterpoint. The meaning lay in the sensations they produced; it could be felt but not captured in words. It was the most creative reverie she had had in her life. What had unlocked that creativity? She was amazed at the power of her imagination.

"College was fun," she heard herself say. After a moment, she added, "We reached for the sublime while sipping lime soda. Foolish dreamers we all were." But she didn't believe it. They weren't foolish dreamers. They had the audacity to dream what was possible. Life had not dashed their dreams to pieces, turning them into cynics. "Your enterprise was a dream. It still is. You're trying to save your dream. And you can do it if you summon all your softness, humour and vivacity—sources of vitality, a necessary ingredient for inspiration and creativity," said an exquisitely tender voice. Divya wanted to embrace it. Where was it coming from? In an instant, the question was pushed to the back of her mind and memories of sweet old days rushed to the forefront of her consciousness. She remembered the wide gleaming smile forever plastered on her lips. She wanted to appear amiable to keep the few half-friends who, feeling charitable, chose to hung out with her. She dressed with great care, trying to look her best, which essentially meant trying not to look fat. She concealed her flab with cleverly designed kurtas that took ages to stitch. She had heated arguments with her tailor, who, despite knowing her triggers, would never fail to remind her of the unrealistic nature of her demands. How could he possibly stitch a garment that would lend shapeliness to a figure that was the antonym of slender—a figure that wasn't elegantly curvy, attractively voluptuous, or, at the very least, fleshy in the right places? He didn't convey that bluntly. He knew how to make his point without actually making it. But Divya would coax and prod him till he had no option but the yield to her exacting, no, excruciating demands. He would jog his brains till his thoughts begin to race culminating in a brainwave. He would note down the brilliant ideas with galloping speed lest they slipped away before he could catch them by the tail-end. He came up with many innovative designs, revealing that he was actually a fashion designer languishing as an ordinary tailor. He was, however, praised highly for his talents and paid a little extra for his exceptional work. His customers abounded and never did he find himself in want of work. Out of all the garments he had stitched for her, Divya was most impressed by a kurta with just the right cut, accentuating her slimmer parts and concealing the flabby ones with a flowy design that billowed so gracefully that you couldn't get even a hint of the bulk that lay underneath. What did she not do to win over Nikhil? But they never became anything more than friendly college-goers. Not even friends. Just friendly. Remembering that one-sided obsession devoid of even a shred of reciprocity made Divya feel the deep sense of inadequacy that had haunted her for a long time. She was suddenly struck by the fear that she was sliding into that same pit of self-loathing stemming from a feeling that she wasn't good enough. The way she was losing control of things, including her emotions, boded ill for her. "No, you're not lapsing into self-loathing, you are dismantling the stiff exterior and the steely interior that made your heart really hard and deadened your creative powers. You need to ease up for your dormant creativity to awaken. You need to smile. You need to shed everything that is superfluous and superficial to discover your true genius." Oh, that voice. It was so full of love and understanding that it made her want to weep for joy. She had found a guardian angel just when she was sinking in a quagmire. "Rescue me, rescue me," she whispered.

For a while, she was suspended between two states: the person she was and the person she could become. Like most people, she had become set in her ways and couldn't resist slipping back into the person she was. She knew this Divya well enough to conduct the business of life without tying herself up in knots. It's another matter that she already was tied up in knots. Still, she felt more confident being her familiar self, who could do a great deal simply as a reflex and sail through tasks with her muscle memory.

She promised herself that she won't melt at the sight of Deepak. To fortify herself from this growing infatuation, she told herself that Deepak was too ordinary to justify such a fixation. It made sense to plunge headlong into love with someone like Nikhil. But Deepak was no match for him. Nikhil was an exquisite creation of God. Sexy enough to set the room on fire, fluent enough to elicit a thundering applause from an excited audience. When he spoke on grave issues—he was a debater par excellence—the listeners would feel their eyes well up with tears. … Divya cut short her train of thought. Why was she thinking so much of her past life, a life she had left miles behind? She needed to focus on the present. And the present demanded that she guard against that mushy feeling that was weakening her. How did it worm its way into her? Was there a chink in her armour? That was something to ponder. But not at this moment. She had to collect her thoughts, reorganise the meeting, and redeem herself by settling it, once and for all, that she indeed was the boss and always will be. So, it was best for everyone to hold their slippery tongues.

Suddenly a thought hit her like an arrow. She was *fidgeting* during the meeting. She never fidgeted. Never. But there's always a first time. Suddenly, she caught the sound of someone chuckling, which morphed into someone tittering, which dimmed into gleeful whispers—sounding like snakes hissing in a chorus.

She opened her beauty box. Wiped her face with the make-up remover. Wiped away the *kajal* smeared below her eyes, a telltale sign of another bout of tears. She dabbed on her cheeks lots of powder, making her face look newly whitewashed. A tinge of rouge would have complemented the immaculate whiteness of her painted skin. She, however, couldn't stand the thought of even a trace pink staining her cheeks. She could not take the risk of letting people assume the pinkness of her face was actually a blush. If that happened again, no one would ever take her seriously (not that anyone did).

She slipped back into her former self: the fiery Divya whose one glare emitted sparks that were enough to put everyone back in their place. No more effrontery. "Oh, the good old days of gallantry" said a voice inside her head, leaving her aghast. She felt like her head had been hijacked by some supernatural force, which poured a spoonful of honey on her bitter thoughts.

She was a bit ruffled but she knew she could handle this. There was no chance in hell she would put up with even a whiff of insouciance.

No one had ever dared to show her the mirror. What? *The mirror.* Wait. Wait. Where did that come from? Her imagination was running riot, leaving her in a cold sweat. It was *Divya's job* to show people the mirror when they were dawdling, idling or making a mishmash of their work. As Divya emerged from her own torture chamber to go for a cup of tea, she found herself humming loudly, "Love me like you do, no, kiss me like you do". Wait. Wait. What song was she singing? She looked around her furtively and knew at once that everyone had managed to catch snatches of the song. She was assailed from all directions by a faint sound suggesting laughter. Before this got registered, the laughter was stifled with gigantic self-control. This was the last thing Divya needed on a dreadful day like this. Her halo was dimming faster than a racing car, and now she had made a complete spectacle of herself. It will be a long time before she could live this down.

"What's happening to me? What's happening to me" The question kept booming inside her head. Suddenly, she heard a baby-soft voice that reminded her of a luxuriously tender pillow stuffed with feathers. It was the same voice she had heard a couple of times. She wanted to touch the voice. "I want to bring you a profusion of joy, profound peace and an inexhaustible treasury of affection. That's what you need." Divya scanned the room to identify the source of that irresistibly alluring sound. Her eyes darted from face to face in a paroxysm of excitement, but she could see no one other than her employees, who were predictably engrossed in their conversations. She, however, noticed that the muscles of their faces were strained presumably with the effort of containing their laughter. As she observed them, an old memory ambushed her. She remembered an incident in school that was too funny to ever be forgotten. She was in fifth class at that time. Their Hindi teacher kept pronouncing Shakespeare as Sexspeare during the entire period. It took all the students' willpower to suppress their laughter, which kept rising to their throats and had to be barricaded by sealing their lips. The moment the bell rang and their teacher got ready to leave, laughter started spilling like a dam about to burst. And it did burst. The timing, however, was not quite right. The teacher still had one foot inside the classroom when the students exploded into laughter that reverberated across the floor, raising the curiosity of students in other classes. This curiosity was stamped out by the stern look on their teachers' faces. It took no less than half an hour for the laugh riot to subside. But the laughter had only subsided; it had not been quelled. So, it erupted in fits and starts during the remaining periods, interrupting the day's lessons, which were drowned out by a cacophony of uncontrollable merriment. Even if one person failed to contain their amusement, the whole class relived the episode in all its hilarity, setting off a fresh round of laughter. Baffled and befuddled, their teachers watched this carnival of mirth. They tried to establish order but by the time the students sobered up, the period would be almost over.

Lost in her reverie, Divya imagined the entire office giving vent to their suppressed mirth the moment she stepped out for her daily ritual of sipping hot chai. In her mind's eye, she saw laughter gushing forth like a noisy stream. It grew louder and louder till the walls began to shake. And then suddenly, the enjoyment seemed to wane. But only for a while. It surged again like a tidal wave. Such was its impact that the paintings (actually framed slogans) on the wall rattled as if assailed by a storm while the cups and saucers slid from the desks and crashed on the floor—everything was turned topsy-turvy by this unbridled revelry.

****

Instead of leaving for her chai, Divya had been standing and daydreaming near the exit. She was visible to everyone in the office. When she turned her gaze outwards and observed her employees, she saw many pairs of eyes looking curiously at her. "There's no saving me. I've been acting so odd and borderline, actually full-on, comical that it would be an uphill task to restore the image I had fashioned with such painstaking effort," she thought with a sense of dismay. Suddenly she heard that soft-sweet voice again. This time she figured out that the sound was coming from within. "Don't lament, my darling girl. Human beings are evolving creatures, destined to change, transform and, at times, degenerate owing to their vices. But you're not devolving into a comical person. On the contrary, you're developing into a more real person who is fallible, wistful, vulnerable. In a word, you're becoming a person from a persona, a face instead of a mask, a multi-faceted personality instead of being the embodiment of just one role. You're more than just a boss. I know it's supremely satisfying to have the designation and demeanour of a girl boss. It makes you feel that you're on top of the world, that you've arrived. But if you've *arrived* so soon in life, where would you go from here?" asked the voice dripping with maple syrup. It was a valid question, and a difficult one too. Divya didn't know the answer, so she kept quiet. She wanted to converse with this voice inside her head, but the voice was so smart and wise (another first for someone who wanted all praise to be directed towards herself) that was out of her depth. The voice continued after a patient pause, "My dear, the only way now is down. Or climbing a whole new ladder. Or reinventing this ladder, so that you don't have to be a solitary figure at the top but can have a team of higher-ups who can share your worries and work on your problems with an equal sense of ownership. My dear, you're on the topmost rung of a dilapidated ladder. It may collapse any minute, and a fall from such a height would be brutal. So, embrace the change taking over you. Change is messy. Change is chaotic. But change also poses a challenge that acts as a catalyst for growth." Divya was spellbound by this voice. She marvelled at the abundant good sense possessed by this mythical creature: softer than silk, sweeter than *jalebi*, and gentler than a mother's lullaby. And yet it— no, it should be "she"—seemed to be made of sterner stuff. She was worldly-wise. She seemed to have bruised her knees and evolved through a trial by fire: a rite of passage everyone undergoes sooner or later when "life happens". She must have had her battles with failure and defeat, drawing her lessons from the crucible of hardship. Nothing less would have secured her the wealth of practical wisdom she seemed to possess. But she didn't make much of it. Jovial to the core, she poured forth her delectable suggestions like chocolate sauce. "Who are you?" Divya said inside her head. There was a long pause, as if the creature was trying to find the best way to reveal something that might spoil the easy flow of their conversation. Finally, the voice said, "I am Love, Divya." Though sugary enough to put sugarcane to shame, the voice was tinged with apprehension.

The revelation threw Divya off balance. What could be more horrifying than the fact that Love had taken residence inside her head when all she ever wanted was to be freed from it! What made matters worse was the deep liking she had developed for this love creature, wherever it came from. "You needed me," said Love, reading her thoughts. "But you couldn't admit it to yourself or to others. Your repressed yearning for love drew me from the other side of the planet to this rather shabby (don't mind, sweety, a gentle prick of reality) office."

"But I am who I am, who I am, who I am," said Divya aloud, forgetting that the conversation was happening internally. Needless to say, she attracted more unflattering glances besides providing fodder for jokes which were shared with great alacrity. Suddenly, the entire office was flooded with laughter that felt like torrential rain. It was a deluge of entertainment that left everyone drenched with delight. Divya decided to skip her chai and resume the business of the day, terrified that the workplace was turning into a circus with *her* in the centre of the ring.

Chapter 6

Saving a Sinking Ship

It was yet another brainstorming session to reinvigorate Spicy Solutions, which had plenty of spite, in the name of spice, but no solution for any problem presented before it. There was a heated exchange on the hackneyed sales pitch. All the employees unitedly and unequivocally demanded a unique selling point that was less lofty and firmly grounded in reality. The sales spiel was a sticking point they couldn't get past, given Divya's misplaced confidence in the power of her words, inviting the charge of being vain and obstinate. "We need realistic goals and achievable promises if we seriously want to turn things around," said Vinay, adding with a pointed look at Divya, "we need the spirit of collaboration, not a command-driven system. God knows we've done our best to follow your commands, but they haven't served the business one bit, nor have they brought us anywhere close to finding serviceable solutions for eminently solvable problems—-a failure that shows us to be extraordinarily inept, which is far from the truth but it won't be credited because of the poor impression we've made on so many important clients. In the name of the Lord, we don't need spices to help businesses revive. We need remedies that reflect practical wisdom, robust common sense, and a firm grasp on the nuances and nature of the businesses we seek to uplift. We need a vibrant blend of regular brainstorming and methodical research. The files we stare at vacantly and sign off cluelessly are an anachronism in this day and age. They should simply be thrown into the dustbin, where they belong. We can bring our laptops for conducting searches and preparing proper documents on MS Excel, MS Word, etc. It's time for us to stop toying with fanciful notions. We can't dish out some magic masala that will instantly bring a business back to life—*there's no magic whatsoever and no need ever to sprinkle serious advice with some goddamn spice.* His final words were edged with scorn—subtle but unmistakable. Divya could feel her control slipping away.

The effect of Curiosity was beginning to wear off. It had mellowed to exactly the right degree—there was just enough of it to ignite a controlled desire for finding feasible solutions. Even though Curiosity was on the wane, Fear chose to keep away. He watched the meeting from a corner, shrinking into half his size lest Curiosity looked at him with exaggerated pity or he got too close a look of the employees who had left him overawed. It was strange to think that he once held them captive. The body of language of the workers announced their strong self-belief, or to put it more bluntly, their rebellious reinforcement of their deflated self-belief.

Fear no more the heat of Divya's temper, nor the frosty look that makes her all aquiver

Someone scribbled this in a flash of inspiration and circulated the chit for the amusement of his colleagues. Well, that wasn't perfectly true. Deepak was ridiculously proud of his adaptation of Shakespearean verse and couldn't withhold the urge to flaunt his ingenuity, which he hoped would win him admiring looks. That didn't happen. The employees read the chit and savoured it, but it was all for their own enjoyment. They didn't care to look around for the composer of those lines. They just tittered noiselessly and passed on the chit for the "greater good", which for the employees meant spreading the cheer by sharing jokes with fearless abandon. The chit took three rounds of the table where the employees were seated in a circle. Vinay, whose vocal cords, like recalcitrant children, could not be controlled, burst into momentary laughter, earning the ire of all his colleagues who glowered at him. Vinay's lapse of self-control didn't get them in trouble though. Strangely enough, it didn't raise the slightest suspicion that some mischief was at work. Divya was too preoccupied with building a defence for her sales pitch that everything around her faded into the background. The voice in her head was too loud to catch any other sound. She resolved to make it plain to everyone that the marketing pitch would remain exactly the way it was. It was non-negotiable even if it didn't go down well with her workers. She made her views clear: Even cutting out a word from that seamless spiel is nothing short of doing violence to both the rhythm and creative vision of my business model. It is no less brutal than lopping off a flower-bedecked branch from a tree in eternal bloom. This pitch is evergreen. It will never lose its resonance. Don't give me that look. It is a great pitch and now it has become our anthem, our motto, the melody playing in our minds as we deal with daily grind. The pitch won't change. Sorry." Before Vinay could edge a word in, she shut him up, "No way. I am wide awake. You need to wake up to the fact that your imagination is barren and your ideas are second-rate. Level up. Come up with something fresh. … Okay, just come up with something, anything. Uff."

"May I say something you don't want to hear," said Basu. It was time for him to get even with Divya for ripping his sentiments to shreds that unforgettable day two years ago. "Your *charming* sales pitch ceased to be charming a long time ago, *if* it had been charming to begin with. My colleagues and I cringe at every word we have to literally force out of our throats. In an instinctive attempt to preserve our dignity, our lips get glued before we utter the cloyingly appealing words that make up your sales pitch. Having repeated the same words over and over, they have started to sound like inanities, *if* they didn't do so to begin with."

Unable to bear Basu's calculatingly cutting words, Divya made a gesture for him to stop. To reinforce her point of view, she described her USP, sales spiel and business model in terms that glowed brighter than sunshine. The sales spiel had lost all resonance, but Divya burnished it with her lively articulation. The employees watched her performance with a poker face, resisting the temptation to retort "Well tried. Better luck next time."

Repetition kills the charm of words. They need creative play and innovative usage to temper their monotonous drone. Once they have been repeated ad nauseum, they begin to fray at the edges, like overused garments. Punctilious editors would have frowned at her uninspired pitch while fashionistas would have marvelled at her sartorial sensibility, which was nothing like her frayed, outworn pitch. When it came to her dressing sense, Divya was beyond criticism, so immaculate was every one of her outfits. Maybe she should have become a fashion designer. This business was a misfit for her insecure temperament. And the sales pitch was the bane of the enterprise.

The employees would inwardly curse the sales spiel as they raced through it:

Spicy Solutions, a business dedicated to supporting fledgling enterprises and languishing retail outlets. This is the business for every business (Oh yeah, sure). That's Spicy Solutions (mumbled in embarrassment). The place where you get what you've been promised (a mocking undertone mixed with guilt). That's Spicy Solutions (tripping over words to get past this repetition). The place you visited not for airy-fairy notions but for perfect resolutions to your business conundrums. That's Spicy Solutions (slurring the words to say it super- fast). Whether it is sunshine or the rainy weather, we always deliver (attempting to not cringe). That's what makes us stand out from the crowd (adding cliché to cringe). Have a problem? Time for a spicy solution.

Deepak had an opinion on Divya's allegedly brilliant sales spiel. That was something to remark upon since he was a man strongly opposed to squandering time in the idle occupation of forming opinions on things and people. When asked why he was so averse to an activity essential to the life of the mind, he would respond with dripping sarcasm, “Oh, yes, concocting opinions is essential to the life of the mind. Without bandying words and adding one’s two cents on every insignificant affair, or prattling aimlessly about someone’s girlfriend or freshly trimmed hair, we would all be brain dead, eh? Thank you for enlightening me. I was under the mistaken impression that our jobs, which demand us to jog our brains and exercise our intellect, were the real source of vitality for the mind. Forgive me for registering my protest and not parroting an opinion whose copyright rests with someone else. Without wasting more of my precious time, let me say it straight: no matter how great your opinion is, it is of little consequence in the cosmic scheme of things. The stars would not realign themselves to accommodate the opinion of insignificant beings like you and me and, for that matter, even the best specimen of our species—there’s a catch there though. The universe is not equally indifferent to those who have scaled the heights of greatness and nobility. Their opinions are presumably accorded a better treatment and rightly so. They don't shoot the breeze at street corners, attempting to pass off their vague impressions and subjective denunciations as well-formed opinions on subjects they only partially understand. The real opinion-makers, whom the universe can spot from miles away, put across their views in a measured way, with every word chosen with great care. They are wise enough to know that opinions carry weight only if they are a product of strenuous contemplation, backed by intense research and validated by vast experience and body of knowledge. Though they are on solid ground, they are open to revision and re-evaluation of their robust opinions. No wonder then that the universe lends them an ear and consequently changes the state of human affairs—sometimes a little, sometimes a lot. Whatever be the case, their opinions make themselves heard. But the rest of us are far below the radar of the mighty forces shaping the world. So, we will do ourselves a massive favour by letting go of the fallacious assumption that the universe is waiting to hear from us. It is NOT. Let me repeat it: It is NOT. Let's do something better than obsess over our own opinions. Leave that to the prophets, the legends and the all-time greats."

When someone loudly advertised their views, Deepak's eyes would glaze over. Vinay, who saw Deepak as his guru, would often feel it his duty to regurgitate the views of his master. Well, it is a fact commonly observed that acolytes, with their zeal to prove their worth, often outdo their gurus. Vinay would launch into a monologue more scathing than anything Deepak had voiced till now:

Yes, yes, you are right, my friend. I am of exactly the same opinion but I couldn't have articulated it so well. You are a genius, no kidding. The universe is taking notes as you speak, and everybody is in awe of your unique ability to stop the clocks till you are done doling out your wholly original views that are accidently shared by everyone else. You must be felicitated for taking such great pains to render into words every piece of your mesmerizingly muddled thoughts. Don't think I'm calling you a muddlehead. That would be better left unsaid and you know buddy that's not even true. You are … You are … YOU. There's no one like YOU. What an honour it would be to be YOU! How skilfully you stitch your thoughts, muddled though they are, into an unassailable point of view. I must add a footnote here: In all truthfulness, this is truly the truth. Your ostentatious display of your dim intellect is matched only by your incredibly vain endeavour to attach enormous significance to your intellectual nonsense. You are the epitome of self-proclaimed brilliance. Who wouldn't want to leave their work and lavish all their attention on you, especially when you are dishing out your eye-opening views! Never worry about validation, my opinionated friend. You will be the cynosure of all eyes in every party you attend. The hoopla you generate around your opinions will be amply rewarded by the bemused wonder of your audience.

To put things in a larger perspective, Deepak made a few sharp generalisations:

I'm ready to bet that human beings brandish their opinions simply to assert their presence. They seek to validate their existence by offering distinct views that prove their unique relevance. Oh, what would we do without people voicing their world-changing opinions—every utterance as flimsy as vapour, leaving nothing solid, in fact, nothing at all, in its wake!

****

Coming back to the sales pitch, Deepak strongly felt that "Have a problem? Time for a spicy solution" spoiled the rhythm of the not-so-great but not-so-bad spiel. He felt it made sense to say "Feeling hungry. Time for a healthy meal" or "Feeling tired. Time for a break". But there is no specific time assigned by the universe for a *spicy* solution to any problem that may present itself anywhere anytime. There was a time when you needed to go on a vacation, a point when you had to focus on weight loss, a time to start preparing for an exam if you aimed to cover the entire syllabus, a time to upgrade your skills to make strides in your career, and a time to rekindle the spark with your partner before your relationship fizzled out with no hope of a revival. But who on earth ever reached that "momentous juncture" when a *spicy* (the word made Deepak cringe) solution was the need of the hour, the decree of the universe, and the source of your salvation. The whole concept of "spicy solutions" was pure bunkum and had to be thrown into the dustbin, no matter how loudly Divya protested, threatened and, not to forget, hollered.

All eyes were on Deepak as it was his turn to share his ideas at the meeting. He stood up and spoke with palpable conviction. He knew his words would trigger every prickly bone and raw nerve in Divya. But he did not hold back. He spoke in a manner that was matter-of-fact, business-like, and profoundly dispassionate:

I am not going to mince my words because we don't have the luxury of living in a fool's paradise. I urge Divya to listen to every word with full attention, no matter how distressing it may be for her to contend with a reality that permits no evasion and that warns us of a catastrophic situation. Very soon, we'll have to shamefacedly shut shop not because we lack talent or the fire in the belly to turn things around. What *we*, or let's be fiercely frank for once: What Divya, and only Divya—no one else shares the blame—lacks is her ability to look at her ideas, work and, in fact, even her commonplace words with even an iota of objectivity and spot the issues staring in the eye, beginning with the sales pitch which will be thoroughly revised, Madam, because we cannot let you ruin an enterprise that has begun to mean something to us and to which we have a sense of responsibility. This will be the sales pitch. Sit down, Divya, and pay attention to the revised marketing spiel. (Divya was too disoriented to notice the temerity and imperiousness with which she was being addressed, and that too by her name). So here we go:

If your business that was once thriving has hit a hurdle for any reason: a slow revival after a lean season; a competitor offering cut-throat discounts to steal your customers, luring them till you're out of business and then leaving them with no option but to pay the real prices of what had been offered as dirt-cheap items; no one comes to the shop and you only get online orders placed through giant corporations that eat up most of your profit margin; your selection of items doesn't win your customers' admiration; you took a loan to buy the shop and the monthly instalments overshoot your earnings, creating a perennial deficit; your business idea couldn't get off the ground, so you're back to the drawing board; and any other obstacle you are unable to surmount because you lack the highly specialised problem-solving skills possessed by a team handpicked by our super-smart entrepreneur: Divya Galore. Welcome to "Solution Finders: We Care for your Business".

Divya, Divya, Divya. For once, just listen to us. Stop squirming, grimacing, writhing, scowling and summoning all your anger to scream your head off. Try to understand that no one was ever in need of a spicy solution. It's a frivolous title and concept. We need to act fast to save a business that is already on the precipice. Before I am accused of mansplaining, I will introduce you to another businesswoman, who wishes to see your business flourish, showing the world the power of a woman leader. Aditi, please come in. By the way, the revised sales pitch was written by Aditi. She was your client long ago and has been watching your business sinking with a heavy heart. She is a believer in woman power and will spare no effort in revitalising this promising business. She wants us to work together and for you to repose faith in her.

Divya's jaw dropped when the simply dressed Aditi humbly entered the meeting room with a genial smile conveying her mild temper and grounded approach. Divya stood up to protest but Love entered her head. It began to release more serotonin to replace anger with joy and flooded her with oxytocin, the love hormone, to slowly transform her aggression into a concoction of goodwill, gratitude, warmth and loving solidarity. "So, what ideas do you have?"

said Divya in the gentlest voice she had ever used for anyone in the workplace.

Aditi began slowly, tentatively, and then eventually got into her stride:

My dear Divya, you went on a completely wrong track. We need smart people and even more than that we need smart women who can navigate a prejudiced patriarchal landscape. But we must draw our lines and avoid the error of overplaying our hand. Moderation is essential even in a frenetic marketplace functioning at a maddeningly fast pace. You've been offering glib assurances to your clients without the clear intent on delivering on your promises, confident of wriggling out of any tough situation through your masterful manipulation. You failed to see the long-term impact of your lacklustre or rather non-existent efforts. That's where you fall short. You need to have a double focus that allows you to meet immediate demands while keeping track of how your performance in the short run will impact your business three or four years down the line. Let your mind's eye have a split vision: one eye caters to the present while the other watches over your future prospects. Your abysmal "solutions" have really dented the reputation of your business. I have made discreet enquiries and learnt that even when your former clients badly need solutions, they desist from contacting you because of their disappointing past experiences. Some of them manage with mediocre consultants, while others have lost faith in the efficacy of expert intervention, leaving their enterprise to fate in a fatalistic manner. Though they've wrapped themselves in complacency, they can't help wallowing in misery. They said that you were dangerously skilled in weaving a web of words that could trap anyone, absolutely anyone. That you should be awarded for this dubious distinction. That's not the image you or anyone would want to have. It could sound the death knell for your business, in all seriousness. Don't sink your own ship by acting smarter than is wise. The day is not far when no word-traps would be able save you from the ruin that was literally invited like a guest. Don't mind my directness but this business is flailing, floundering, and finishing itself. You have a smart team. I have told them to level up, taking every assignment as a test of their mettle. For the next one month, I will be getting you clients on a daily basis and widely publicising our achievements and successes. Trust me, even in that little period, the business will be back on its feet and clients will start coming on their own. You just have to keep up the momentum. You will go from strength to strength from hereon. Believe me, sister, we can do this together.

By now, love had reconfigured Divya's brain. She went to Aditi and gave her a long, tight hug. "Yes, we can do this together. With a sister like you, I have nothing to fear."

Epilogue

"Making love inside your head," said Divya on finding Deepak fantasising during work hours. The moment she said this, her cheeks turned a blushing pink with a reddish tinge of embarrassment. Deepak was jolted out of his raunchy reverie. He was surprised to see Divya looking mortified, giving him a shy, somewhat sheepish, smile. The business was now being run differently. Aditi's painstakingly accrued entrepreneurial knowledge had begun to uplift the enterprise fairly quickly. The atmosphere in the office was more relaxed, yet more focused. As Deepak gave Divya a swift, sweeping look, he noticed the change that had come over her. She seemed less stiff; her face wore a natural expression; and her gleaming eyes were a window to her authentic self. Unencumbered by her heavy armour, she was a vision of loveliness. Looking at her deepening blush—his scrutinizing glance made her lose all her self-possession—he blushed as well. They communicated something wordlessly, though neither knew what exactly had passed between them. Whatever it was, it left an afterglow.

By now, the effect of Curiosity had begun to wane and other emotions rushed to make a place for themselves. Those emotions excluded Fear, who had been traumatised by the power of Curiosity. He couldn't stay in a place where he had been rendered impotent by the cheeky, bitchy Curiosity. Horror was watching the proceedings from his hiding place because Love had spread its fragrance everywhere. Even a whiff of that fragrance could make Horror faint and fade away. He found a hiding place that had not yet been invaded by that "poisonous" perfume. Divya had stopped hollering and the employees had stopped chatting about it. It had been three whole days since anyone had even whispered the word "holler". For the shallow Holler, this was a steep drop in popularity. The place had changed into a suffocating cage where everyone spoke so gently that it made him want to holler in frustration. He was too flighty to wait and watch what was in store. He packed up his stuff and was off. It was a "calamity" he had not suspected because, as you know, he was not far-sighted.

Impish was caught between a sense of having a place in the new order of things and a foreboding that he was not going to fit in. Had Impish lived up to his meaning, denoting cute, childlike naughtiness, he would have fit snugly into this place. But he had changed for the worse. He had turned into a spoiled, self-congratulatory brat who openly made fun of others. He didn't care a fig for anyone's feelings. In his attempts to break into the realm of the dignitaries, he had become unscrupulous and deceptive. "I have strayed too much from my definition and become more suitable for darker regions. I will be soon thrown out for being an impostor, which is not what I am. I am a deviant extraordinaire, and I don't belong in this despicably ordinary, suffocatingly dingy place. So, let me find greener pastures where I can liberally spread my newly acquired darkness." Deep down, Impish wanted to stay, but he was terribly scared of his dark layers getting revealed. His insouciance was a cover for an identity crisis. The actual plan, which he hadn't even admitted to himself, was to swiftly escape and find other representatives of the word Impish. They could help him rediscover himself, making him feel comfortable in his own skin once again. It was too difficult for him to be honest about his self-inflicted misery. He had to give things a positive spin or else he would have grabbed his head and cried for a century. He regretted mocking the blameless trio of Impecunious, Imperturbable and Importune. They never meant him any harm or harboured any grudges against him. He wanted to go and hug them before he left. Luckily, he found them wandering near Divya's office. He rushed and embraced them all at once with his exceptionally long arms. The three were too stumped for words. Before they could say anything, he slipped away, turning once to give them a salute.

While the words were puzzling over their place in a place perfumed with Love, Divya and Deepak were lost in a deep kiss, cheerfully violating the office protocol. Love had decided that the sooner she banished the darkness in this place, the faster the light would make it nice and warm. So, she poured out all the softness in her to melt the remaining hardness in Divya's heart. She would need to fill herself up again but that could wait. First, she wanted to watch the impact she had had.

When the kiss was over, Divya said to Deepak, "I wonder why love didn't come to me sooner. I feel like a garden blooming with flowers. All this while, I was no better than a wasteland—hiding its barrenness, watering it with anger, cursing it with scalding tears. I reviled myself more and more with the passing years, living in the eternal fear of being shown the mirror. Even if I tried to smile, it never came from my heart and shone in my eyes. After so long, I feel happy. Truly, madly, deeply happy."

Deepak paused to hold the delicate thought before he said lovingly, "You are reborn. You now have *everything* needed to rebuild this business. Make it something brilliant. Let the genius in you finally emerge."

"Yes, Boss," said Divya with a sunny smile, suffusing the office with a shimmering light. Suddenly, the whole place resounded with applause. The employees had been watching the goings-on with rapt attention. They laughed. They winked. And they gave the lovers teasing smiles. After so long, they experienced pure delight.

Horror and Holler were nowhere in sight. But there was light. And love.